LOST&FOUND
IN QUAIL LAND

Gladys Villalobos

WESTBOW
PRESS®
A DIVISION OF THOMAS NELSON
& ZONDERVAN

WestBow Press books may be ordered through booksellers or by contacting:

WestBow Press
A Division of Thomas Nelson & Zondervan
1663 Liberty Drive
Bloomington, IN 47403
www.westbowpress.com
844-714-3454

Because of the dynamic nature of the Internet, any web addresses or
links contained in this book may have changed since publication and
may no longer be valid. The views expressed in this work are solely those
of the author and do not necessarily reflect the views of the publisher,
and the publisher hereby disclaims any responsibility for them.

Any people depicted in stock imagery provided by Getty Images are
models, and such images are being used for illustrative purposes only.
Certain stock imagery © Getty Images.

ISBN: 978-1-6642-5461-9 (sc)
ISBN: 978-1-6642-5460-2 (hc)
ISBN: 978-1-6642-5462-6 (e)

Library of Congress Control Number: 2022901900

Print information available on the last page.

WestBow Press rev. date: 02/08/2022

To the memory of
Sean Florence Quilter.
In your kind and encouraging words
You said to me:
"Don't stop writing, don't stop painting,
Don't stop your art."
I listened and followed your advice.
I feel blessed to have met you

CONTENTS

Chapter 1

IN THE MIDDLE
OF NOWHERE

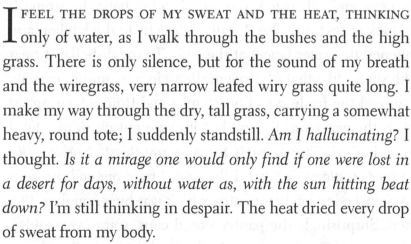

I FEEL THE DROPS OF MY SWEAT AND THE HEAT, THINKING only of water, as I walk through the bushes and the high grass. There is only silence, but for the sound of my breath and the wiregrass, very narrow leafed wiry grass quite long. I make my way through the dry, tall grass, carrying a somewhat heavy, round tote; I suddenly standstill. *Am I hallucinating?* I thought. *Is it a mirage one would only find if one were lost in a desert for days, without water as, with the sun hitting beat down?* I'm still thinking in despair. The heat dried every drop of sweat from my body.

I blink and blink, realizing it is a house surrounded by grass. *It's not my imagination*, I thought in relief. I stopped, looking at the details. It looks gorgeous; a porch with large white columns made a fence supporting a nice roof over it. The unkempt yard and ivy covering part of the walls led me to believe no one lived in the house and no one was living there. As I get closer to the steps, I notice weeds everywhere and the paint peeling. I slowly continued to walk up the four steps and found myself on the porch. I look through a window, trying to get a glance on the inside. I couldn't see much besides furniture and rugs because of the curtains but managed to see some. By common instinct, I pulled the chain hanging from a bell by the door and said out loud, "Hello!" I tried to open the door after no one answered. I couldn't open it. I walked to the other three windows; there were three windows by the porch; I found one unlocked by the left-side extension of the porch and let myself inside.

Besides the layers of dust and spider webs, everything looks nicely placed, some spider webs. I remember being so thirsty, hungry, and exhausted, starving. I didn't have the strength to look at anything else; I walked directly to the kitchen and opened the water faucet at the sink. To my disbelief, I hear the sound like that of a waterfall, a glorious sound, making you feel the freshness of water mist and think of spring. At first, the water was brown, but it came out clean as I let it run. I'm drinking enough to calm my thirst. *Nothing like water to settle one's thirst*, I thought. I then opened the door to the wooden kitchen pantry, which was big enough to fit a bed. Surprisingly the pantry stored cans, soups, vegetables, tuna, meat, flour, sugar, and salt, nicely organized and very dusty. At this point, I can think of anything else but invite myself to a feast, setting the table; fortunately, there were table cloths, kitchen towels, silverware, and lovely china. After eating beans, vegetables, and meat from the cans, "I better wash my plate and put things where they belonged," I said out loud.

I try to turn the light on, but there seems to be no electricity. The refrigerator door was left open, obviously intentionally, as if the last person living in the house was planning to stay out for some time. I make my way to check the breakers box. So far, it feels I'm living a hallucination, or maybe the heat was getting to me. *There is power!* I thought, astounded by the cranking sound, like a car that wouldn't start, of what appeared to be the Air-Conditioning trying to kick on. I'm slowly making my way through the living room, dining room, and office room with books, nice chairs, an ottoman, and windows overlooking the trees. I could gratefully and to my content, see the lime trees, shrubs, grasses, and other flowering wild plants.

I continued my way through the three remaining rooms; each one had a full bed, nightstands, chairs, and empty closets, but one had a man's clothes—, casual clothes, working clothes, and shirts for a medium-sized man. I decided to lay down in one of the other rooms, didn't bother to take my sneakers off, and stared at the chandelier hanging from the roof. My eyes closed.

I was startled awake by a constant hitting noise coming from the roof, something banging. I couldn't tell how long I had slept. I took a look at myself in the mirror; *a shower is in order*, I thought, by my appearance. So, "into the shower, it is," I said softly. *It feels good, so good*, I thought. I took clothes out of the round pack I carried with me, *my things*, I will assume. Loose, comfortable pants—, I seemed to feel comfortable in loose clothes. I got a sense of freedom to move and to breathe, same as my shirt was flexible and a larger size. I found a pair of worn-out loafers in the bag. I pulled my hair up, wishing it were short. A ponytail would do. I set to dusting and cleaning up work. I listened to birds chirping, the noise in the roof had stopped, and there was some a hot breeze and the whistling sound of leaves.

By the end of the day, I had only dusted and cleaned the living room and the dining room. Looking at my day's work, I was astonished to have found this house with the classy decor in the middle of nowhere with such a tasteful décor. However, the furniture was heavy but of good quality and design. The cozy, laid-back, Royal blue sofa caught my eye. It gave me a welcoming feeling, so comfortable, I thought. There were two tan flower-design chairs, a center table, Accent tables, etc. Foot lamps, even though the ceiling had, in contrast, a rustic chandelier. I went outside for a bit. The sun was setting; it was a pleasant view. The first day had ended. I had something to eat, took a shower, and went back to staring at the chandelier until my eyes closed. I later awoke to be awakened by what I definitively confirmed as a woodpecker. I saw it flying fast with a squawking sound.

As days went by, my cleaning and dusting kept me busy —too busy to try to find out if there was a town somewhere close nearby. I became absorbed by the house and tried to learn to whom the house belonged. I decided to leave the reading office room for the last. It gave me a feeling of invading someone's intimacy while simultaneously calling me in, which scared me some. It was the only room displaying photographs —a little girl and some dolls. Every time I went in, I would trip over a piece of old wood on the floor, which made me decide to try to fix it., I found it a more challenging task to work at later.

I went out and continued with the back closed porch, which had outside furniture stacked, such as chairs, rugs, and tables. Surprisingly, I found myself thinking *it would make a great work table for me. But why should I think of a work table?* In the following days, I moved some furniture to the outside porch, making a nice place to sit and relax while enjoying the outdoors, relax and enjoy. So that's what I did.

While I was taking a break from my house-cleaning activities, it occurred to me I should try to go back to the place where I'd had the accident. I only remembered being scared, confused, and feeling dizzy from obviously a bump on my head; with a rock; my body was half -inside the car with my arms and head out, resting on the rock I must have fallen on. I'd grabbed the round bag by the front seat and just left running, not knowing who I was, nor how I'd ended down in that ditch surrounded by shrubs, high, dry bushes, and longleaf pines., and as I got out of the gutter and I'd started walking at a fast pace and then, I came across the land with bushes and lime trees. It was very dry, though.

It occurred to me, *why didn't I think of that before?* I thought. *I should try to go back the way I came in. Maybe I can find the car and get my things and some information that will lead me to find out who I am.*

I have no rush; this peaceful ambiance has captivated me. Although I do need to find out if there are neighbors, how far away, what kind of people live around me, and what is the closest town. *So many uncertainties!* I kept thinking unsettled.

I will finish with the back closed porch and then get me some gear to find the car. What about the office room? I should also need to try to clean the office. It's dusty, but it will give me a clue of the house; after all, I am trespassing. The thought of the unknown and the office, or rather the reading room, gives me a creepy feeling which intrigues me. *I might as well finish what I started*, I thought.

I opened the windows and started dusting, admiring several accent tables scattered around the room with pictures of the same little girl. She was slim and had light hazel eyes, blonde-brown hair, and a charming smile, petite.

Two chairs were placed side by side by the window— and a bookshelf with books from top to bottom. When I started dusting the shelves, some dust fell in my eyes. I moved back, tripping by the desk, and knocked the desk chair down. I picked it up and sat on it by the desk. Once I dusted it, I noticed a key taped in the middle of the desk. I figured it would open the desk drawer, and so I did. There were papers and an envelope addressed to -*Your good fortune* - I was stunned; *what did it mean? Who would leave an envelope addressed like that? Should I open it?* I wondered.

From the moment I got out of the vehicle, confused and scared, it has been so unexpected, so unpredicted. *I am invading someone's property! Why is this happening? Who am I?* On impulse, I opened the envelope and started reading.

"My name is Edward Darwin, owner of the property. If you are reading this letter, it means you made your way into the house. I cannot stay in it any longer. I don't know what my future holds. I wish that the house serves as a shelter for someone who can tend to it and make it a home. I honestly wish that whoever you might be can be fortunate enough to value and care for it. Edward Darwin, July 16th, 2009."

I am in tears; I don't know if my tears are out of sadness or contentment. I folded the letter, put it back in the drawer, locked it, and put the key in a chain pendant I wear around my neck. I finished cleaning the reading room, my mind was blank, closed the window and left the room not without tripping again, *a sign I should fix it*, I thought.

Another day went by. I worked with a feeling of uncertainty. At this point, more than ever, I have the urgent need to find who I am. I went outside, grabbed some limes to make lime juice, had some dinner, and went on to make plans to take a walk, hoping to find the car and shed some light on my identity. I made it thru the night slightly relieved, or not, and some strange feeling is taking over me. The sound of the woodpecker wakes me up. It is now, officially, my waking call. I started packing some food, water, grabbed a hard stick, a knife, and left, trying to remember how I got here and follow back; after all, it hadn't been so long, maybe three weeks.

I started walking and got to the area where the grass was tall and dry, bushes tangled, softwood forest; after a while, I encountered open space, more grass, a pond with brushy borders. I went around it into a longleaf pine forest with an open floor covered with wiregrass. I had walked about half a day, and luckily summer was fading and was not as hot as about three weeks earlier. Back then, I was confused, scared, running in despair. Unexpectedly the sound of a loud gunshot startled me, birds suddenly shooting into the air and a loud dog barking. I didn't know what to do at that point, the barks sounded closer, and I could also hear steps on the dry-wired grass. I saw the image of a man holding a rifle wearing an orange vest, a hat, and a dog running past me, sniffing for something precisely without stopping. A harsh sound of something falling from the sky, and the dog came running back to the man with the orange vest, who was then almost in front of me. He noticed I was shaking and confused because he immediately introduced himself, trying to calm me down. He was caressing his dog dropping the bird from his jaw. It was a quail. I had a bitter-sweet feeling.

The man said, "I am Michael Lamont, miss. I probable startle you. I always come around this part of the woods for quail hunting; after all, this is quail land. What are you doing around these parts? You certainly don't look like a quail hunter nor equipped for it."

"Good boy, thunder! He is my hunting friend, a great hunter, and friendly too." He continued. A *beautiful dog*, I noticed. It seemed a good breed, white parts and brown spots and a pointed nose wagging his tail. It sure made me feel at ease. So I replied;

"I don't know my way around these parts." Before answering, *I remembered the words in the letter Edward left in the desk drawer.* Words just came out of my mouth, "I managed to get to Edward Darwin's House, not knowing how, after I lost control of my vehicle and ended up in a ditch about three weeks ago and went running scared and confused. That's where I'm heading, trying to see if the car is still there and recover my belongings".

I didn't want him to know I didn't remember much of who I am. Protective instinct, I thought.

I added, "Oh, how rude of me. I'm Lindsay," the name just popped up out of the blue. "I am not sure where the car is nor if I am heading in the right direction. Maybe you could shed some light or direct me".

Michael replied, "I'll do better than that; I have a feeling I might know where a distraction can take anyone, especially a stranger to these parts, out of the road. There is a tight curve towards the rural areas leading to plantations where some live and some just come for pleasure and hunting. Edward Darwin has a small plantation, but I haven't seen him in about a couple of, maybe more, years. Good to know someone is there. We take pride in these lands and try to keep the spirit of good neighbors and good hunting. The closest city is Thomasville, about 50 minutes south".

Michael wouldn't stop talking and kept on saying, "Well, Lindsay, why don't I bag this quail, and I drive you around that curve? Who knows, you might be lucky. And we'll take it from there. What do you think?"

I would certainly accept your hospitality; you are a savior. Thank you," I said in relief.

On the walk to his vehicle, Michael didn't stop talking. I learned about quails, how those beautiful birds prefer open country and brushy borders. The hen lays about 12 roundish eggs in spring, which the male may help incubate. The young remain with their parents the first summer; how quail eat mainly seeds and berries and take leaves, roots, and some insects. I became involved in his chat, so much that

I became intrigued by the idea of eating some quail flesh which, according to Michael, was a delicacy. I also learned that wiregrass commonly grows in this area, sometimes called the -Wiregrass Region- after this distinctive and persistent grass species, most seen around pine forests.

We got to his vehicle, a truck, not surprising for a hunter, large enough, with coolers and cages. He put the quail in an ice cooler, where there were several already; thunder jumped right in after his command, followed by me. I hoped my instincts wouldn't betray me; I am too in compliance with his hospitality. The hunting class went on; his voice faded to my ears as I dazed back to thoughts on Edward Darwin and Michael kept on. I kept on thinking why he would have left these lands, call it a Vacation spot or retreat, just like that. Not too far into our drive, Michael pulled to the other side of the road, drove the truck out of the road, and stopped. He pointed out the curve.

A very tight turn, and all you could see was tall grass, bushes. Traces of bushes knocked by what appears to be tires, cars, we had just come out of a road with bushes and tall longleaf pines side to side of the road and into the curve. We got off and walked towards the edge when I tripped on some branches, slipped, feeling I was going down a slide. Hit my head with a rock, Michael rushed down. I just heard rustling and thunder barking. Michael helped me up; although slightly dizzy, "I'm fine," I said. I see flashes of me in the car, trying to gain control of the vehicle and not stop until it hit a large log on the grass. I told Michael I was sure the car was somewhere close. We walked some more, getting closer to the longleaf trees, I remembered. Michael stopped me and noticed thunder had silenced, pointing his nose still, bushes blocked our sight; we could only see thunder. Then the rustling and quails like rockets into the air. Michael was disappointed because he didn't grab his rifle; he would have made his hunting day; at the same time, it led us to the car, where some quails had sheltered underneath. A fallen tree stopped the vehicle. The door was open.

Michael then told me he would call his friend at the shop to come and tow it. In the meantime, he went to get his truck and drive it closer, and I was able to get my things, my handbag with my wallet, ID. *My name is Lindsay Reed from Minneapolis, Minnesota*; I read it on my DL. There were bank cards, some money, bags, and to my surprise, art tools, rolls of silk, and PVC rods … I couldn't make much sense of it except that maybe I had an art hobby. I found my cellphone on the floor of the front seat. It was getting close to sunset. We finished loading the truck and headed back on the road.

Michael's friend would call to let me know the situation with the car. I had to wait to get the phone charged once back in the house; then, I would learn more about who I am beside my name and where I was heading. Michael mentioned I'd be surprised at how close Edward's house is back on the truck. It was like a 30-minute drive listening to Michael bragging about how lucky I had gotten into open land with just high bushes and a log on the way. Of course, the quail class kept on. I could certainly feel his pride in the land, dog breeding, hunt, quail, deer, and ducks. He pulled out into a small road and a wire fence and a wooden sign - The Darwin's - He got off to open the gate; the road covered with dry grass, it took about 15 minutes in when we came to the back of the tool shack, and around it, the house.

Why didn't it occur to me to look for a road or gate? I thought, embarrassed. We went in to freshen up and calm our thirst, not without me expressing on and on my gratitude to Michael. He rushed to help me bring my things inside the house. At this moment, I want to be on my own. Michael has been more than helpful, I thought.

"I understand you might be tired. I am anxious to take my things out and start organizing. I can't take more of your time", I said, to what he gracefully replied, "not only that, I have overextended my hunting day, and I'm sure Agnes, my wife, is stressed out, probably called several people already. I know that woman; it wouldn't surprise me if she comes knocking at your door tomorrow and wants to boss you around, don't get me wrong, in a good way. We are hospitable folks around these parts. I best be heading home. Why don't you check your phone? You did plug it, right?"

"Yes, it's the first thing I did when we walked in," I answered. *That's something else to thank, Edward.* I gratefully thought. I was surprised; once I pulled the breaker, the power went on.

"I just wanted to share numbers so I can let you know what Ben says about your car," Michael said.

So we shared numbers, and off he went.

After Michael left, I took a shower. I felt unsettled, agitated, and anxious, put on loose sweatpants and t-shirt, and started walking from one side to another. Opening bags and boxes, hoping to find a clue of who I am or expecting one of the boxes to talk to me or slap me to wake up from this nightmare. I was feeling more and more anxious, uneasy. I started crying desperately. For the first time, I felt lost. I gave a few spins and said out loud, "Ok! Stop!" Stretching my hands, arms, I rubbed my face, took a deep breath. I started chatting to myself. "Let's do this, make a nice cup of tea and go thru my things slowly; no one is rushing me."

I moved the oversized ottoman closer to the sofa and emptied my handbag; it looked more like a shoulder strap tote bag with pockets. "Talk to me ... talk to me ... please, say something," I kept saying while going thru the things. The only thing I have learned to this moment is that I left Minneapolis, driving from Minnesota all the way south to Georgia. *Is Georgia my final destination? Did I know Edward Darwin?* I thought. I continued randomly, taking things out. Nothing familiar, except my eyes, focused on a black bag, zippers, wheels, more like a carry-on traveling bag. I was nervously shaking but grabbed it, unzipped the front; there were several manila folders, one containing a lease agreement to an office space in downtown Thomasville under my name Lindsay Reed – doing business as Whispers, a 12-month contract. I remember Michael mentioned Thomasville being the closest city, 50 minutes away! *Did I know Edward Darwin?*

I kept reading the lease, "to engage in the art and craft business." *Am I an artist?* I thought in surprise. I gave a two-month deposit and paid three months in advance starting on September 1st. 2012. The realtor's name signing read Susan Carter. So, it came to mind; I *was almost at the end of my trip. Where was I planning to stay? So many questions,* I kept thinking. I put the lease away pulled out another folder, several blueprints of apartments. – "I was planning on renting an apartment," I said out loud. I opened another folder. Divorce documents! *I am a divorcee,* I thought. It makes some sense; I divorced and was probably on my way to creating a new life, maybe or maybe not. Reading on; Lindsay Barnet vs. Robert Barnet. – I changed my name! My Driver's License reads Lindsay Reed. *I'll open one of the bottles of wine Edward was kind enough to leave in the pantry; I am glad I put one in the refrigerator. What kind of a person am I?* I thought. I poured some wine in a glass and went back to the living room to the divorce papers. - savoring the wine. I didn't realize I had a taste for wine until this moment. Reading on, no children involved, we did share a house from which Mr. Robert Barnet bought my half. Some furniture and paintings to me, along with vehicles, the SUV I had the accident. I kept the art and craft business – Whispers- and the account related to it. Divorce finalized June 2012.

It was already midnight, and I was tired. Not a light on my memory was coming back. I finished my wine and went to bed to be awakened by the phone ringing. It was a tune, part of the classical melody, but it frightened me. I didn't know if to answer it or not; I looked at the time, it was 7:00 am, who would call so early? I start hearing loud voices in my head, screaming at me, calling me a man's voice. I'm feeling well; I'm getting anxious, breathing heavily. The music stopped. Images came to mind of the bottles of medication I had in the bag. I got up fast to get them. The living room was a mess of half-open boxes and suitcases and papers. I did see the bottles and, on it, a name of a doctor who prescribed it. Dr. Linette Stewart. A place to start. I also had the cell phone, which I seemed to have ignored unconsciously, maybe afraid of what I could find. *I should look into it!* My instinct told me.

I'm getting hot flashes, perhaps anxiety. I went to the kitchen, made some coffee. By then, it was 8:00 am. I retook a shower and heard the tune, the phone. It made me nervous; *I should change it,* I thought. When I answered, a female voice asked for me, so I replied: "yes, this is Lindsay." It was Agnes, Michael's wife -" Michael told me about your encounter yesterday, are you alright? I just want to know if I could go by and pay you a short visit, it is not good to be alone in strange lands. I would love to help you know the area and take you to town". Again, *I could not thank them enough,* I thought, and of course, I said "yes," but I also expressed to her I had lots to do organizing and going thru my things, so we agreed she could come by around 4:00 pm. I feel I need someone to talk to, hoping she wouldn't talk as much as Michael.

I'm still uncomfortable and uneasy, so I called Dr. Stewart. I grabbed the phone and dialed the number to Dr. Linette Stewart; as I started pressing the numbers, I felt a fresh mist, the kind you feel when you walk by a large water fountain, and an image of a large, cheery came to mind.

Someone answered, "Dr. Linette Stewart's office, hoy may I help you?"

I replied, "I want to speak to Dr. Stewart, please."

The voice at the other end replied, "I'm sorry, Dr. Stewart is with a patient right now. How can I assist you? I am Melissa, her assistant".

"Could you please ask her to call me? My name is Lindsay Reed", I said.

"Miss Reed, how are you? How was your trip to Thomasville? Are you already missing Minneapolis? I would certainly ask her to call you," Melissa, with excitement, replied.

Melissa? She didn't give time to say anything else, I thought, but said –"Thank you, it's important."

I don't know what to do, *what would anyone in my situation do?* I thought. "I might as well move the boxes and bags out of the living room to the back porch" talking to myself. I made myself some toast with cheese and coffee, and started tidying the living room for Agnes' visit this afternoon. I was hoping time would pass fast and Dr. Stewart would call me. I'm not being able to do anything else, I went outside.

Chapter 2

FLASHES OF A
PAST LIFE

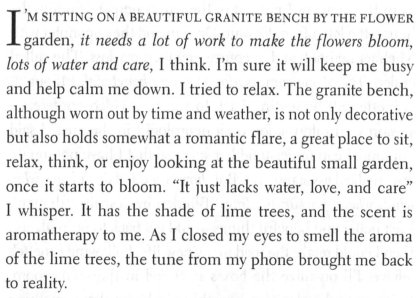

I'M SITTING ON A BEAUTIFUL GRANITE BENCH BY THE FLOWER garden, *it needs a lot of work to make the flowers bloom, lots of water and care,* I think. I'm sure it will keep me busy and help calm me down. I tried to relax. The granite bench, although worn out by time and weather, is not only decorative but also holds somewhat a romantic flare, a great place to sit, relax, think, or enjoy looking at the beautiful small garden, once it starts to bloom. "It just lacks water, love, and care" I whisper. It has the shade of lime trees, and the scent is aromatherapy to me. As I closed my eyes to smell the aroma of the lime trees, the tune from my phone brought me back to reality.

"Hello"! I quickly answered while I walked back inside.

"Lindsay! How are you? I hope you found everything as expected and ready to shine". It was a friendly woman's voice.

I was holding my tears, and words came out with difficulty. "I don't know who I am or what I am doing here; I was hoping you could help me remember;" my voice is breaking, getting faster, agitated. I continued "All I know is that my name is Lindsay because I read it on my driver's license and that I'm divorced because I read the dissolution papers."

The woman's voice interrupted me – "hold on, what's going on, calm down, and let me ask you, what do you mean you don't know who you are"? "Lindsay, this is me, Linette!" astonished.

The voice is that of Dr. Stewart. I'm letting Dr. Stewart talk and I'm beginning to feel comfortable enough to call her Linette. It's been almost thirty minutes on the phone, Linette listens quietly as I'm able to describe everything in detail, from the moment I ran out of the car in despair, finding the house, the letter from Edward Darwin and the encounter with Michael Lemont, and of course, my memory loss. The called ended. *The phone conversation was very beneficial,* I thought. "Linette will be getting back to me in a video conference session with information on a neurologist in the area" I said out loud. I can understand her surprise that I have not sought any medical assistance yet. But, *how could I? I don't know who, what, where, my surroundings!* Blinded by despair, I thought. I felt better and hopeful things would get back to normal, and then I could retake the road to my new life. Following Linette's advice, I'll organize the boxes scattered in the living room, trying to find a place for everything in hopes that something would make me remember.

What type of a person am I, what do I do? Why did I choose to come to Thomasville? What is here for me? I guess asking myself all those questions would not bring my memory back.

I'm standing looking at my tasks back in the living room. I moved every art supply to the back porch; for some reason, the back porch seemed like a good art studio. There are PVC tubes, pins, tapes. *What would I do with that?* I wondered. A box of dyes, brushes, rolls of silk all went to the porch. I sat for a bit by the ottoman filled with notes and receipts which came out from the bag when I emptied it, trying to find a clue. My eyes focus now on a yellow paper, which looks like a receipt. "It is a receipt for a moving Company from Minneapolis to Thomasville to arrive by August 20th," I read out loud. *It is August 5th*, I thought looking at the date on my cell phone.

I have to start getting ready for Agnes' visit, something to add to my list of questions for her. Close to 4:00 pm, already showered and dressed, I have nice loose pants and a summery top; I am feeling tired, but I managed to put most of the empty boxes in place and even got a key lime pie out of the oven. The rest of the packages would have to wait.

Cling Cling Cling! I Love the sound of the bell by the door; it announces Agnes had arrived but to my surprise, *or maybe not*, I thought, Agnes found her way inside, the first sign of a nosy person. "Lindsay is me, Agnes!". As I walked to the door, she was already making her way to the living room. "Hello Agnes" I greeted, I didn't make eye contact with her but with the scarf she wore, and everything is going slow motion, colorful, for some reason it brought colors, soft cloth, smooth like silk around me until "are you alright?" Agnes said, "Oh yes! I'm sorry, didn't mean to stare, I couldn't help staring at your beautiful scarf"! I candidly apologized. She took it off and let me touched it; surprisingly, the touch, the softness, felt very familiar, and I saw myself creating designs to drop dyes in silk, later on, giving life to some art creations. Quietly I'm trying to enjoy the moment without alerting Agnes of any possible problems with my mind and went on telling her that my business is art, crafts, oils, and, most relevant art on silk. I felt such a relief.

Agnes sounds delighted to hear me talking with such enthusiasm. This time I seem to be leading the conversation. For a short time, Agnes remained quiet, listening to me. Until she started telling me that her friend, Susan Carter, is a realtor meanly for commercial listings, had told her she rented space by the downtown district to a new artist coming to town; what a coincidence, "could that artist be you?" Agnes asked.

I could indeed picture Agnes snooping everywhere; nothing escaped her! I thought.

"Well, Agnes, it can certainly be me. I have to get in touch with my landlord; I believe her name is Susan Carter." I replied, as I remembered the lease I found in the black case, "not only that, I have scheduled movers to deliver my supplies and furniture to the rented space." I added.

At this point, I seem to be creating my new life with the bits and pieces putting them together.

I asked "So, dear Agnes, you must have lots of lady friends and know many people in town. I hope you don't mind me taking advantage of your hospitality and asking you for a tour around Thomasville, even showing me my new business place".

"Of course!" Agnes candidly replied.

Agnes looks older than me, with white hair, light blue eyes, and very slim but tall, which made her scarf fall with elegance and dark red lipstick on her fair skin—dressed casually, slacks and bottom blouse short sleeves. I offered her all I could think of, tea, coffee, Lemonade, wine. There, she stopped me and said "a glass of wine will be great".

"Red or white?" I asked.

"Red", Agnes replied.

I got up to get the wine followed by Agnes, who continued to talk, just like Michael, about how she would plan a gathering with her lady friends to welcome me, which to me sounded perfect. I jumped in to ask her to wait until I got the store settled, and we could use the opening as an excuse for her to invite her friends. Besides, September is just around the corner. Agnes offered to give me a tour of the town and indicated the best places for shopping, groceries, bakeries. I meant to ask about Edward, but I am afraid she'd discover I don't know much about him, even though I am eager to learn what he does, why he left, but for some reason, I avoided the subject.

I 'm trying to concentrate on talking about visiting the realtor, visiting the store. At the same time, Agnes just keeps asking about me, why I left Minneapolis to come here if I had relatives. Two glasses of wine later, she left, leaving me in a proactive state.

I went to the reading room, opened up my computer, which I have already set up at the desk, and started browsing for myself; *Lindsay Barnet*, I typed, many came out. "Let's narrow my search to Lindsay Barnet, Minneapolis," I said, "and let's add artist" with a wink. A list popped up and images; "how can anyone get lost? Hmm, Lindsay, you sure made it easy to be found as Lindsay Barnet" I said in a witty remark. There was enough information to keep me busy and learn what I could do in my "new unknown role" as a business owner; *I must have done something good* I thought triumphant.

A ring tone! Message notice! Mail coming in. I hesitate to click on mail. I get up and start sweating, anxiously walking from one side of the room to the other, tripping again by the loose floorboard; "ouch! I got to fix that!" I screamed. The ring tone is banging in my head so much. I'm seeing images of that big cherry; this time, the cherry sits on a giant bent spoon, and water sounds like splashes when hard rain falls, I can't make anything of it, thought of the meds again. *Still, Linette told me no take them lightly* I thought, so I just better try to relax, taking deep breaths, "how are you going to find yourself if you panic every time a new light pops? Get a hold of yourself!" I keep telling myself.

Back to the computer, no reason to delay it, *emails it is*! In my mind. Most emails are from suppliers, services, notices of bank statements, not much personal. "Hmm, Do I have any friends?" I say softly. *Weird,* I thought. It wasn't that scary. *I will go to town as soon as I get my car ready,* I thought. I better get things in order. My memory has to come back! It's getting late, and I need some sleep. I got up, left the room, and went to bed. My eyes closed soon after staring at the lamp hanging from the ceiling.

The room feels dark, and I find myself getting out thru the window running scare, but I heard a loud voice in rage calling me; I try to cover my ears, the voice scares me, but I hear it louder and closer I turned my head to see if it was near, and it was, about to grab me. I recognized the face; I woke up sweating, I realized it was a nightmare. Still, I remembered the face in the dream; it was Robert, a rude, disrespectful, recalcitrant man I had feared for many years and whom I finally left. I saw a flash memory of me getting in the Blue SUV I had the accident weeks ago. It's all I can remember. I got up and went to the living room, and Just as Linette had suggested, I focused on getting my life organized with what I knew at that point.

The computer held a lot of my information, enough for me to create my new life, but at the same time, the fact I didn't remember things made it difficult to access my information. So far, I'd learned I am an artist, I own a Self-Company, I have online presence, I just rented a space for an art and craft store, *everything is so surreal,* I thought. *I'm in a house authorized to live in, and I didn't even know the owner.* At least I remember who my ex is to stay away from him. After a while, I realized I had to go to the bank to use my account on the computer. The annoyingly unpleasant sound announcing a call made me jump in horror and, at the same time, brought flashes of me walking by a lake where I saw the giant spoon; I seemed to be late; I'm walking at a swift pace. I answered the call; it was the mechanic announcing the car was ready. He offered to bring it over, but I will have to drive him back.

Things are starting to fall into place; *I know I will finally remember, my memory will return, it will be much better* I thought in self-confidence; in the meantime, I got ready to get my car and go to the bank. Making time while waiting for my car, I started cleaning the back porch. I began to assemble the PCV tubing into a long rectangular frame of about 64 x 12. After I did it, I sketched some cherries of different sizes, like the ones in my memory flashes, and kept trying to figure out where a giant spoon fitted in; instead, I just added water drops and lines.

I lost track of time; I felt drawn to getting the dyes out and setting up everything on the long table. I got the role of silk out when the sound of my car's horn honking got my attention, and I left the roll of silk, grabbed my handbag, and went out to meet Ben, the mechanic who arrived in my car. I rushed out; as I did, I felt the cold mist of water, and I remember my walks to Linette's office as well as driving to the Attorney's office overlooking giant sculptures. But Ben required my attention; getting the car is essential, and now I feel more resilient that my memory will come back as my new life moves on. Keeping active according to the original plan and the flashes of familiar scenarios were slowly leading me to my past and new life. Right now, I like what I see around me. I feel energetic and eager to continue creating what I'm starting.

Ben greeted me with a huge smile, a friendly mechanic in overall, tall, heavy build. "Hello, Ms. Lindsay," Ben said, "I got your baby ready and in good shape, waiting for you to drive it." – "Fantastic Ben, I'm thrilled" I replied to his greeting.

We agreed that it would be better for him to drive back to the shop since I didn't know my way around yet. That way, I could enjoy the ride and the conversation, and so I did.

Ben told me he would drive to his shop located in Thomasville, using the back road to avoid some traffic; by doing so, I could enjoy a better scenery of the quail land. Like Michael, he was talkative and definitively showed his pride for the land, most of all, the hunting. He mentioned the back road is called the "plantation belt" because of the quail flight patterns between plantations along the south of Georgia. There are vast plantations, now lodges and resorts for hunters, not only for quail but pheasants, turkeys, deer, guesses. The land assured an abundance of quails.

I feel delighted, it's a road with longleaf pine on both sides of the road, and of course, I couldn't have asked for a better guide than Ben. I 'm learning those longleaf pines allow some sunlight to reach the forest floor allowing thick ground cover, wiregrass, and broomsedge, a weedy grass that gives protection and food quails need to survive. Now, every plantation in the area is getting ready for the hunting season starting in the fall, and they would be expecting lots of visitors.

When he mentioned Mr. Edward Darwin, I took my eyes off the site to turn to look at him."Mr. Darwin is a photographer; he is not a hunter, nor tried to be one, but went along with the hunters to take photos, not only the birds, but the dogs, lovely pointers, great breeds, and loved ones. Which, by the way," Ben kept on. "now that you are in his house, I will bring you a puppy. Mr. Darwin left his dog, a female, until his return. Unfortunately, she died of old age but had puppies, which grew. I always kept a female, and more puppies came along. I have a puppy ready to give away. It's tough for me to care for him. – Joy was the name of Mr. Darwin's dog. Didn't Edward tell you about his dog?" he asked me and said, "It was his little girl's, not really hunter, but a playmate" – I replied, "I must had forgotten. A dog will do me well, I need company, and I love dogs".

The conversation stopped at about a 40-minute ride, we were in Thomasville. It had been a pleasant ride. At the shop, after paying, I asked Ben to direct me to the bank, so I drove off to the bank to get my finances in order. It wasn't hard to get to where I wanted to go. Driving made me feel confident, as if I knew where to go and what to do. *I probably researched before choosing to head down to this place and rent a business place*, I thought. For some reason, I know what I'm doing. At the bank, I was able to update my information. I took Edward Darwin's letter as a lease contract and gave that address. I realized I could have done my business with the bank by phone, but presence is essential for business, and I'm glad I came. I met the manager, Jonathan Levin. I came to Thomasville with financial backup from half the proceeds from the house sale in Minneapolis and a business account under Lindsay's Whispers. I'm already in the car calling Susan Carter, the realtor who gracefully agreed to meet for lunch, and then she will take me to the final place, "my store", I said.

Driving on my way to the place where I would meet the realtor was pleasant. Thomasville surprises me, a lovely city, the usual nationwide franchises, stores, and familiar businesses. Somehow, it didn't take me long to get to Historic downtown, so I parked and decided to walk and admire the place closer. Certainly southern feeling! Few people were walking around, but cars parked along both sides of the street. I found the restaurant and Susan Carter was waiting for me at the door. Susan, nicely dressed, friendly smile as she greeted me, and not surprisingly, Agnes had already given her head start on me. After asking if it was easy to get there, we walked in. I noticed most of the tables taken, soon we were taken to a lovely table for two by the window.

I had done my homework before taking this trip. I signed all the paperwork and paid the required deposits. This lunch was more like a social networking thing; I just needed the keys to the place. As a courtesy to me, Susan would take me to the store. She turned out to be a delightful lady, middle-aged, very professional, and friendly. The food was excellent, local cuisine. The fact that everyone I've met is so talkative gives me some relief; I don't need to talk about myself nor what made me come here. However, so far, I have been able to answer questions without any problem. I'm glad no one has asked about Minneapolis. It happens when people are so proud of their city, I guess. Sometimes I wonder, *too hospitable, too friendly, so far so good.* Things will slowly fall into place.

I offered to pay the bill and no problem there. We left the place and walked across the street where lovely small shops were further down and a sudden stop. - Here is your store – I was stunned, out of breath for seconds, as Susan opened the door. I was just looking at the empty display windows, one to each side of the central green door, the canopy awnings. I then remembered my store back in Minneapolis, "Whispers," the silk scarf is flowing, the pillows, different sizes, it was like a tornado of colors; I was there and me, right in the middle of it. I laugh so loud, so happy, and I run inside, remembering why the silk, the dyes, and the store. I stopped in the middle of the empty store, so amazed and happy, and I cried tears of joy. I hugged Susan, "what do you think?" she asked.

–"It's just as I expected, it just needs to –be dressed-" I answered.

"Another happy client" Susan replied and went on, "here is the list of service suppliers; you can start getting the place ready, so you can open on the 1st as you planned, right? Now, I have to leave you; remember I mentioned meeting a client and it is almost time. Don't forget to lock on your way out".

"– Of course, thank you so much, Susan. We have to meet again and wait for the invitation to the opening" I said as she was leaving.

Alone in the store, I already know what to do. I have a to-do list on the computer already planned. I was overwhelmed with all the information coming to me. It sure need to get to work. I spent time in the store, checking and making sure things were in order; there were two bathrooms in the back, the main store shaped in L plus two good-sized rooms. To the far right of the store, there is my office workshop with a glass overlooking the right front side of the main room and next to it to the left with an open arch to the left side of the main room, art workshops for students' children and adults. I then remembered my furniture arriving on the 20th. So I need to have the store ready by that date. After a good hour and a half, taking notes, envisioning the final design of the place, I went out, locking the door, turning to look at the store, walking back to my car, and driving around the main road towards "Darwin's" plantation, home. I'm thrill, super excited, eager to get to work, and the main road would be more direct.

As I am driving, I noticed fast-moving traffic; I'm a little apprehensive, don't want to lose my exit towards the house. I'm getting anxious; it feels like a panic attack coming. I'm near the exit, which leads to a minor road with longleaf pines along the way, meaning I'm on my way, but I feel scared and the loud voice calling me names started banging in my head, and I can't make it stop. I'm at the exit making a left turn, I'm now on the minor road leading to "the Darwin's plantation, but I can't keep driving. I have to stop on the side of the road, or I could risk another accident.

I'm crying desperately, asking myself, "why I let that man tear me down and almost destroy my self-esteem, always nitpicking and criticizing others; his excessive rage blowing up in a blink for no reason. Never, never for one second did he apologize or say sorry for insulting me, humiliating me, and always blaming me for everything. Why oh! why?"

I'm so mad at myself. He is so conceded, he thinks he's so intelligent, and is just a recalcitrant, pathetic, disrespectful nobody, expecting I drop everything I had going just to run like a puppy to assist him. "Why, oh why didn't I stand up? What kind of a person am I? Who do I think I am? What am I doing?" I kept repeating as the voice inside me kept getting louder again.

"I tried to talk to him; he wouldn't let me constantly interrupt; it was more important to talk about his day. I didn't have a saying" I'm in rage.

I got off the car to get some air and cry more. *When I met him, he was sweet, charming; he seemed family-oriented, just to be surprised by his obnoxious use of words and loud voice to order me around. Why didn't I react? Love faded; I stopped loving him. Did I ever love him?* I thought.

I started hating the way he chewed his food, his heavy breathing, his gestures. Every time he talked about my family, it was to insult them. "Oh, Linette, I clearly remember you, and I have so much to thank you" I say in relief looking up to the sky. *It was such a daunting job I imposed myself thinking I could change his pathetic, toxic character—what a waste of a life, what a waste of years,* I thought as I dry my tears and said out loud "What would I have done if I hadn't had my passion, art, in my life?" I took a deep breath, got in the car, and continue to drive away—

"No need to cry anymore. I'm back!" I say in confidence and feeling empowered. "This is now my ride to a new life, and I made it. Nothing will stop me now".

"I will make it work" reinforcing as I got closer to the house, to let go forever, the toxic life and the narcissist who almost ruined my life.

I'm back in the house. I ran directly to the back porch, grabbing the silk I had stretched where I started to outline the cherries, and, just without mercy, I tore it, ripping the silk in rage. The images of the cherry and giant spoon taunting me all this time are those of the Spoonbridge and Cherry, a piece of modern art. The cherry stem is a fountain spraying water into the spoon bowl and the pond. The sculpture is a Minnesota icon in the sculpture park in Minneapolis which I walked and drove by every time I was on my way to Linett's office and later to the Attorney's office. After letting go of my rage, I called Linette, there was no answer but I left a message to call me back.

I took a long shower, it is already early evening, and I'm starting to feel a weight off my shoulders. I grabbed a glass of wine and sat outside to relax as a truck drove in. It was Ben.

We meet again. I'm here to bring something that belongs to this house. Ben opened the front door of his truck. The most beautiful white with black spots puppy dog jumped out of it, wagging his tail as if he came to a very familiar place, right up the front porch, sniffing me, everything else around and sat by the door—long silky fringes on the back of the legs and the tail.

"This is smarty, it's time this house has a dog again. His mom was an English setter, but Darwin's little girl wouldn't let anyone train her dog for hunting but to be her best friend, so maybe you should do the same with this pouch, in her honor, where ever she might be. Maybe one day she'll come back and find a dog, like when she was a little girl, she's a woman by now; last time I saw her, she was about six years old" Ben said.

I thought of the picture, the only photo in the house, a little girl. Ben continued saying, "and the last time Darwin was here, he didn't bring her with him, nor his wife. It was just him, alone. His two boys didn't come with him, the two boys were older and kind of spoiled, but the little girl, she was like an angel, her daddy's little girl".

"Would you like to come in and have something to drink and stay for diner?" I asked Ben. I'm trying to see if he would tell me more about Edward Darwin.

"I have to run back, I do accept the drink" Ben replied.

I'm looking at Ben as he drives away leaving smarty behind who had no intention of going anywhere. He sat by me, put his pointed nose on my lap, and allowed me to caress his head.

When I finally got up to go inside, he jumped right after me, and inside the house, he came running, sniffing everything and then, followed me around. Ben left his bowls for water and food, his sleeping pillow, his food, and a few toys, the little girl had left for the dog she once had. I put the bowls on the floor by the pantry and filled them up, one with food and the other with water. *The house is now sheltering a lady and a dog!* I wonder if I should look for some other place to live; after all, I wasn't counting on this property. It was my original plan to rent a place to stay until the business picks up; then why don't I? I looked at Smarty, he moved his head, wiggled his tail; what was I thinking?

The phone rang, I answered. "Hi Linette" I said. It feels so good knowing who is calling and not being scared. *What a relief,* I thought.

"How are you doing, Lindsay? I hear a happier voice" Linette replied.

"Yes I am happy, it so happens that I now know all there is to know!" I said in excitement. "Everything makes sense, Linette. I can't thank you enough!" I went on, "I did have a panic attack and it was then I remembered. I had the crying spell I often had at your office, but I'm now calm and relieved".

"Focus on your life and remember that it was your passion for art, perseverance, and courage what made you who you are,—a strong woman" Linette reassured me.

"That's what I plan to do, and although I know the mystery of Edward Darwin is still a puzzle to complete, the search is going to wait for a little. I now have a Store to open and a lot of work ahead. Before I get to that, I need to feel I have left trouble waters behind and be able to focus on my store. I need to stop the tears; enough is enough. I need laughter, joy." With that in mind, the conversation with Linette ended. I grabbed a cup of coffee and with smarty went out to the porch.

I'm sitting on the porch, it rains. The animals are sheltered somewhere just like me. It feels good, as if everything stops, leaving idle time to watch the rain hitting the leaves and the rocks, creating puddles of water. The lovely sound brings such a pleasant, restful air; it invades me. Life hasn't been bad since arriving at this area, making it my home, and discovering, day by day, someone once lived under the roof of this lovely house in the small plantation -the Darwin's-, who one day decided to depart, leaving it behind to whoever was lucky enough to find it. *How can I not be grateful?* I thought. As I stare out at the rain, *let the garden in my soul bloom by day and let the flowers whisper to each other and giggle,* and caressing smarty's head I look at him and I said out loud "Mr. Edward Darwin, has to wait. I have lots to do, -Lindsay's Whispers- my store will open soon".

Chapter 3

THE STORE

⁓

THE LIGHT HITTING THE BACK PORCH WITH THE FULL MOON enlightens me; the workshop slowly gets in shape. Dyes are in line on the shelf, ready for me to grab them and give life to pieces of silk. The nights are peaceful, the sound of nature and my selection of soft classic tunes flow inside me, and I spend hours creating. Quails hiding between branches, hunting dog running, and tall longleaf pines will come alive in cushions, scarves, lamps, anything that comes to mind. *It is almost 4:00 am; soon, it will be dawn when I finish the last piece. I escaped from reality, and into my world, I go!* I think, reminiscing what my life has always been, waking up in the middle of the night, walking into my art workshop, and continuing where I left off before going to bed or starting a new project. It is like traveling to unknown places where I alone can go. Watching the dyes do their job on silk was surreal but real. Then, waiting for the colors to set, going thru the steaming process made me forget about real life and feel alive. My eyes needed to rest. I went to bed feeling satisfied with the night's task. Thanking the moon for bathing me with the energy from its light, I fell asleep.

The waking call, the woodpecker is back; this time, it made me jump out of bed full of energy. I should give the bird a name! The drummer, that's it. "Good morning, drummer," I said. I took a shower, dressed in working clothes, I always end up with dyes all over me when I work, so I have my special outfit: a very loose top and loose pants. The smell of coffee brewing took me to the kitchen, had some light breakfast, and started getting the pots ready to steam my night's work. "Oh no," I said. I just remembered my pans are coming in the moving truck arriving on the 20th.

Many artists buy expensive steamers; I used my tools to do it—large pots, with the canister at the top to steam vegetables. "When there is a will, there's a way," I'll figure it out; that's an essential process in silk artwork, setting the dyes, so the color never washes off. *I could hang it outside, letting the heat from the sun rays set the colors, but I risk having the color fade in time or at the first wash,* I'm thinking. I then went to the back porch and started unpinning the stretched work and wrapping it in newsprint paper, then in aluminum foil. The amount of work I did would require several pots for fewer hours. By mid-morning, I still had my calls to make when the tinker bell sound delighted my ears, accompanied by smarty's barking, which was already by the door when I got there. *Surprised, not other but Agnes!* I thought. She acted surprised I had the door locked. I said I wasn't about to sleep with the door unlocked. She nodded!

"I'm on my way to town, though you might want to come or need something," Agnes said after greetings and a good morning hug.

"Well, hello, please come in," I asked, and she followed me to the back porch, where she was amazed by my organized mess, for lack of a better word. She was curious.

"What are you doing?" Agnes asked.

I explained to her the need to steam my artwork to set the colors; to do so, I had to buy at least two steamers. I accepted her invitation to the city; it would allow me to purchase the steamers I need; I can't afford to wait until the movers arrive on the 20th. But I also have to make some calls to start running the store services. I always had all my tools at hand and did everything on my own to get my work ready, so asking for help or accepting help was new to me. Agnes turned out to be a noisy but friendly and kind person eager to give a hand.

Agnes said– "No-nonsense, Lindsay, I have steamers at home, small and large, you can use them, I can call Michael and ask him to bring some to you, would two large ones work? I don't understand steaming your artwork like vegetables, but I guess you know what you are doing. And I can also help you with your services".

I feel embarrassed to accept help, but I need to get inventory ready beside the ones coming with the movers. I already have my designs for display and a new list planned with motives from the area. Agnes was very responsive to my ideas and excited. When I mentioned I would be offering classes for silk art, she seemed very excited. I took a box out to show her some of my latest work before closing my store up north. She was delighted and immediately called Michael to bring those pots right away.

"Let's see – what else would you need?" Agnes continued. We served ourselves some coffee while waiting for Michael. I showed Agnes the list of service suppliers Susan gave me, plus I asked her if she could recommend a carpenter for the front counter, some shelving. All the notes and sketches I took at the space were beneficial. An electrician too, I had my idea for lightning in the store. Not surprisingly Agnes, was ahead of me with carpenter and electricians, ready to call them. I'm feeling her excitement in helping me. I grabbed my laptop and opened the store file with the list of things, furniture, and inventory coming in the mover's truck, not to overdo what I needed right now to continue with my projects for the opening. My joy is overflowing as I read out loud, "box with lamp shades tools" – I can't wait for nightfall to get to work on silk again. I also opened Lindsay's Whispers store folder showing all the store pictures; Agnes was delighted; we were acting like school girls excited about a project. I started showing her and describing everything, so now she has an idea of what I am dealing with, home décor, fashion, and fine art. We were in a pre-work mood when everything was beautiful, and we envisioned a Rodeo Road street in Beverly Hills type of store. I don't see why we couldn't picture it like that, "aim high for success" great motto. In all our excitement, we were interrupted by Michael and the steamers.

"Hello ladies, what are you cooking?" Michael asked.

To what laughing, I answered, "not quail, I can assure you," accompanied by smarty's barking.

"Well, Lindsay, You will soon come to our house to enjoy a nice dinner – local cuisine," Michael replied.

"I am looking forward to it," I said after thanking Michael; I filled the pots with water, turned on the stove, placed the wrapped silk on the top canister, covered it, and let the steam do its work, setting the color. Both Agnes and Michael looked at each other, not understanding what was happening. I told them I would be letting it steam for about 2 hours and then do the other half of work. Michael left, and Agnes decided to do some shopping, not without telling me she'd be back to watch me unwrapped the steamed silk. *It's turning out to be a fun project,* I think excited.

Left alone, "Ok Lindsay, start making calls," talking aloud, starting with the utility services to set up things at the store; then I will contact the carpenters and electricians; I hope they will do their job as I expected. "I don't see why they wouldn't," talking to smarty. I was still under the energy flow, so I went back to sketches, dyes, and silk, music in the background, and it all came to me. It's amazing how art and music play such an essential role in my wellbeing, helping me stay focused, keeping my mind away from despair, soothing my spirit, and enhancing my soul. The most exciting part and the reason I grew a passion for the art in silk is watching the drop of dyes falling from the brush to the silk, letting the color bleed into the fabric and spreading, finding its way in my creation, giving it a dreamy shiny look. Still, I am leading; I tell it when to stop. Right now, all is chaos, pots steaming, silk stretched in different frames, bottles of dyes, brushes, sponges, everything will soon find the calm because that's what it's all about, finding the peace within the chaos and creating harmony, oh! Energy overflows.

The lovely sound of a tinker bell by the door and the door opening distracted me. It was none other but Agnes and a friend who both walked right into my back porch. I got up to greet them. Agnes introduced her friend, a lovely sweet lady, Giselle, who happened to be another neighbor from a close-by plantation, also a lodge for quail hunters. After meeting Agnes for coffee at the mall, she got curious about my work and future store opening and decided to stop with Agnes on her way back home. Although slightly embarrassed by my organized mess, I felt flattered by her curiosity; "if it makes sense to anyone but me," it's what I told them.

– "Nonsense Lindsay, we are happy to be here," Agnes said cheerfully. We then ran to the kitchen, I had left the pots steaming longer, adding more water, so now I'm sure the color has set. Turning off the stove and taking the wrapping silk out, all eyes on it, I couldn't but smile. I took all the wrapping to the back porch, where I had managed to set the table for it. I started the unwrapping process, ensuring I saved the aluminum foil and newsprint paper for the next batch. Giselle took the initiative to help with that. Getting the silk out all wrinkle but dry, loving how it was coming out, most of the themes and designs are quails, longleaf pine forest, hunting dogs, just how I wanted it, and the ladies were impressed. The next step, washing it, making sure no color would fade away, letting it dry a little longer, iron and ready to go to the sewing machine to become the final product; whether it is to be for cushion, lampshade, handbag, scarf, "name it!" I said.

I went on wrapping the next batch for the steaming process. Once in the kitchen and feeling hungry, I brought out some tuna salad I had made earlier, sliced some tomato to make some caprice, with mozzarella cheese, basil leaf salt, paper, and olive oil. I sensed Agnes and Giselle were ready for some good girl time, so I brought wine out! In the meantime, I would let the steaming do its work. I didn't want to brag too much about my work; I will let the final result show it. They both asked questions, and I answered, there would be cushions, lampshades, tapestries, screens, matching scarves and handbags, and more. One can always create anything from a piece of silk, even jewelry. Life is not only –silking-, and the girls started the gossiping part we all love, but this time I was slightly skeptical, afraid they would bring the Edward Darwin subject, from whom I know nothing about, except what Ben let out to me on our ride to Thomasville. Luckily they were more interested in my life; why did I move down alone?

– "Hey girls, silk is my passion, I don't need the distraction, and I am happy how and where I am at this stage in my life," I said. They are under the impression, Edward Darwin rented the house to me, no need to know the details. They talked about their circle of friends, most of the men retirees, with investments in the area; the celebrities that come down during hunting season, and they thought my store could be a good place for the ladies to visit while the men go on their hunting run. However, women also join the hunting parties. The girls got up to leave; Agnes mentioned she contacted a carpenter and the electrician. They would be contacting me.

"Good to know, Agnes! I was about to call them," I said.

Another day went by with lots going on for me, between silk, dyes, steaming, planning, and running to the store for meetings with the carpenter and electrician. The carpenter is very diligent, following my ideas just as I expressed them, and he is also very friendly, making me laugh a lot. I learned he had his own company as an architect – Jeffery Hill –and he entered the woodworking business when he retired. *No wonder he understood me so clearly and gave me some good ideas.* Jeff and I have started occasional lunches together, here and there. I enjoy his company. Jeff used to go hunting around this area and found it so comforting and relaxing he made it home. I had a chance to talk to him about the screens I make and how I had a carpenter back in Minneapolis do the three panels' frame, which were plain painted wood, "you will be able to see them when the movers arrive," I told him. Luckily it will be soon, and there will be more work ahead. With that in mind, Jeff decided to invite me to a relaxing day at a national park close by for fishing and the enjoyment of wildlife, using as an excuse that the body and mind need to relax to perform well. Who could say no to that? So I gladly did. It has been a very long time since I had an outing day; I could say never had but always dream of a day just enjoying nature without being anxious and afraid. *There's always a first time, and never too late*, I thought.

It is Sunday, August 17th. A bright summer day with a breeze and no clouds in the bright blue sky, my waking call, drummer, never missed, I got up, put on some classical music and made coffee, took a shower, and just as I had dressed and put on my shoes, the sound of melody whispering bell announced Jeff is at the door. As I opened the door with the sun hitting my eyes, I could see the tall figure, medium body built, salt and pepper hair, a short beard nicely styled, and the good morning smile.

"Good morning, come in for coffee and English muffins," I said. I was getting ready to pack some water and snacks, but Jeff interrupted me, saying, "I took care of it," so off we went. An adult couple in their late 60's out to an encounter with nature.

He drove through the green forest. A small river stream to the side of the road attracted my attention. Jeff indicated that fishermen would find a variety of fish, including largemouth bass, flathead catfish, crappie, and redbreast sunfish, adding, "this is not the place I'm taking you but to a park where the brackish waters provide excellent fresh and saltwater fishing." The scenery was already peaceful, and an array of ideas for my art projects flowed in my head. Just like Michael and hunting, Jeff kept talking about nature, fishing, the park, getting me involved in all the details until we arrived at the parking place; not many cars, but it was early. He got two fishing poles, a small cooler with bait, and a bag pack, and we headed to a trail into the park—what a delight. I heard a familiar sound, the red-cockaded woodpecker. With great enthusiasm, I said, "there's a woodpecker, my waking call every day since I arrived in Darwin's House." He laughed and told me visitors commonly see a wide range of wildlife and birds. We arrived at an accessible dock for fishing overlooking a picnic area, the river shoreline, and a boat ramp with easy access to the river, where we were heading. A boat and the water awaited!

The boat had another cooler with ice, water, towels; I

had bragged about my swimming abilities, so there were no lifesavers. But there were two pairs of very high boots, ha! Fishermen boots. Jeff paddled for a short while to a creek shore, and there, we got off. It was terrific; the fishing class started between jokes, laughter, and amicable conversation we got into the water. The water was cool and refreshing, wearing hats to prevent sunburn, a cross shoulder bag with bites, and a place for fish if caught. Jeff throwing the fishing line made it look so easy, it took me a while to finally throw my line far enough; Jeff had already fished a few, but nothing like when I felt something pulling my line, and me screaming like a teenage girl, *how embarrassing I thought*, but it is a fish. I caught a fish; now, the lesson is to pull it out and not let it go. It was a wonderful experience, and even more, Jeff got all the utensils to get the fish ready to eat, the fire ready, a nice salad from the ice cooler, and two glasses of wine. It was relaxing and soothing, indeed. After a couple of glasses of wine, eating everything like "cats," a few exchanges of looks, we cleaned up to head back, with a sense of tranquility, brought by the scenery, the water, the breeze, and the excellent company.

"Thank you for a delightful day," I said.

"I appreciated your willingness to get there and grab the fishing poles, hold a fish with your bare hands with excitement like a pro, and enjoy the meal," Jeff replied. "A perfect companion for a fishing day," he added.

Back at the house, I invited him inside to wash and take a look at my back porch. He saw the hanging silk ready for the screens awaiting the frames to turn into an excellent décor room divider. We both had some fresh lime juice, and we both thanked each other for a great day. He assured me as he was leaving, "I will have my work ready by the day the furniture arrived," which was only two days away. He couldn't but notice my evident joy and over-excitement.

I didn't work that Sunday night; I took a nice cold shower and sat out on the porch with smarty sitting by me, contemplating the beautiful moon feeling the energy emanated by the light and the blinking stars giggling at me, feeling a peacefulness never felt before. It was late, and I went to bed, falling asleep right away with the satisfaction of a well-lived day.

Monday and Tuesday went by so fast; I had chosen a neutral color for the store's interior walls to make the colorful artwork stand out. The shelves were perfect brown wood, and the cashier counter came outstanding, classic, and elegant. I couldn't hide my satisfaction, and I hugged Jeff thanking him for his incredible talent and super well-done work. Agnes came in at that moment; we both looked at each other, knowing what to expect soon enough by Agnes's look and expression. We both knew there was a warm friendship growing but nothing else; I wasn't contemplating any involvement in my life, but the art on silk, my business, and I think that the same goes for Jeff, who I know so little. Still, he seems a sound manner, nice, friendly, handsome man who loves the outdoors, nature and makes me feel safe. Agnes had come by to let me know she placed my invite for the store opening in the local newspaper, which will reach out the two following weekends before the opening on Friday, September the 5th, at 5:00 pm – 9:00 pm.

The waking call on Wednesday drummer's serenade, with it, came my expected day; the movers will be arriving sometime mid-morning, according to tracking. I decided to grab my laptop, dressed in working cloth and drive early to have breakfast somewhere close to the store. I found a close-by breakfast café, parked right in front of my store, and walked to the café. A friendly voice greeted me; I got used to the contagious hospitality, making me feel welcome. I was not a stranger anymore; I saw people chatting, enjoying a good breakfast to start the day. As I walked to my table guided by the waitress, someone waved at me; Jeff was sitting with a group of 3 more. I walked passed stopping to say good morning, and he introduced me to his friends, who happened to be store owners nearby. I had a good breakfast, and after paying and tipping, I walked to the store, sights with excitement. I am getting nervous by mid-morning, with no sign of the movers. I worked on my inventory based on the information in my files and cleaned the bathrooms. Johan, the electrician, placed the lamps illuminating the wall space for the wall art, and it looked good. Everything was ready, just waiting to take form; soon, the store's character, Whispers, will show its splendor. The sound of an incoming call brought me back; the mover was a block away!

Two crew started downloading boxes, placing them in the workshop-class assigned area. The first piece of furniture coming down was my desk which found its place in the office where I am sure I will spend hours of productive, rewarding work. The rest followed, chairs, sofas to be dressed with cushions, accent tables for lamps with beautiful silk shades, buffet tables, mirrors, and more. After downloading, I signed the number of boxes received as I packed them before I left Minnesota, and they left.

I am sitting at the office trying to figure where to start. I jumped *right here, in my office.* I moved the work table and stool facing the glass window to the front of the store and the guests' chairs, making it a welcoming office. I run to look for the laminated mats to place under my work table and stools, knowing how dyes will probably drop to the floor now and then. I then opened the folding tables for the classroom workshop to place things out of the boxes and find the final destination. Reading the inventory list and the box numbers made it easy for me to distribute everything. I was merged in my task when the sound announced someone was coming in. I had forgotten to lock the door. It was already 4:00 pm, and I hadn't had anything to eat; I couldn't let anything stop me. It was Jeff, apologizing for not coming earlier to help, but I gladly welcomed, and while I continued unpacking, he followed, listening as I got things out and helping find a place. The computer, printer, and cash register came out; even though I had labeled all the cables matching the connections, I had no patience or knowledge to connect them, art tech is not my field of expertise, and time was against me. Jeff managed to find a home for those gadgets. Close to 6:00, another visitor, Johan, came by to check if the lights were working correctly; knowing the furniture was arriving today, he couldn't stop Aisha, his wife, from tagging along. Aisha was curious and turned out to be another friendly, helpful lady.

Jeff and Johan had become good friends and worked together on many projects. It was still halfway. At least the computer and Register was running, but it was time to call it quits for the night. Johan was able to set up the alarm. Jeff and

Johan put the boxes containing the sewing machines, frames to take home with me in Jeff's truck. Aisha offered to come back tomorrow to help; she was in her 50's I would say; her friendly and gentle attitude made me ask her, "do you work?" to what she replied, "not at the time," so I said, "why don't we talk tomorrow, I'm going to start looking for someone as my assistant with the store". She smiled, saying, "I do some freelancing as a Public Notary and accountant; in fact, she handles Johan's accounting." "Well," I said, "wouldn't you like to add me to your list?" I have a feeling a friendship is starting.

Days went by with the feeling I had a giant sand clock in front of me, watching the soft sand falling through the small opening, waiting to empty the top telling me everything should be ready to open the door of my fairy tale and to make everyone be part of it. I worked day and night from the day the movers arrived, making sure nothing slipped my carefully planned details for a magical stage, choosing my best products. I wanted everyone to feel silk as I do, a soft, brilliant, light material that will fall naturally at one's touch.

Johan did a great job with the lamps' socket lines, and the different lamp shades were coming out just perfect. I spent days at the store and nights at my back porch swing cushions, painting, steaming, and creating. Aisha and I worked together and laughed at every idea we came up with, which was not bad. Dressing the two windows became another primary task. I place one of the love seats and the mannequin of a lady sitting, wearing a beautiful silk scarf and matching hat. Another love seat housed two cushions, one large with a longleaf pine forest design and a hunting dog running, and a smaller one with a couple of quails flying. The accent tables with lamps matched one of the pillows. I was getting ready to place one of the screens to one side of the love seat when Jeff walked in the store, surprising me with a beautifully carved three-panel wooden frame for the screen; it was a work of art. He took the screens off the existing wood divider I had and placed them on his; it was beautiful. Another business venture for the store was born, wood and silk. *Jeff, Johan, Aisha and I did a good job.* I thought.

The Magical stage is ready; the audience is entering with the sound of gentle jazz music. Legend has it that Circa 2,640 BC, a Chinese Empress Leizu discovered silk when a cocoon dropped into her teacup. She began to unravel meters and meters of silk fiber and dreamed of weaving it into cloth. I have become enchanted with this art form. I'm dazzled by the magic of silk's translucence. My store is devoted to making you love this art and its forms. Whispers look radiant; there's red and white wine at a cozy bar located in a corner by the entrance so guests can savor it as they walk and view the different forms of art and a comfortable classic bench to sit and admire wall with wrapped silk art. Everything feels magical. The cash register hasn't stopped sounding along with the music!

The night is happy, the moon shines, the stars glitter, a moment of silence, Johan, Aisha, Michael, Agnes, Jeff, and I left in the center of the stage, and of course, Agnes broke the silence; it has been magical! Lindsay, you should feel proud; I am happy to have you as my neighbor, cheers to that, said Michael. "Whispers," the store, is now officially open.

Chapter 4

AN UNEXPECTED VISITOR

⁓

I T'S THIS TIME OF THE YEAR WHEN RAIN FALLS ALMOST EVERY day. I love to watch the rain, listen to it as it hits the roof, the trees, and it's always nice to reminisce. Three years ago, I celebrated the re-opening of Whispers, the store. Today I'm wondering about the girl who ended up on the steps to the porch two days ago. The noise of wood cracking from the old wooden floor took me away from staring at the rain and reminiscing about Mr. Darwin and how I made it to Darwin's plantation and what life has been since. September rain in 2015, I turned to look at Maryann, who, after eating, cleaning herself under a nice warm shower, and resting, looks different from two days ago. Like a scared, wounded animal, Maryann ended by the doorsteps, in rags, dirty, sweaty, very afraid, and begging for water and seeking help. Maybe now she would feel ready to share who she is, something more than her name, what happened to her that made her end up here like I did once. *Could she be related to Edward Darwin?* I wondered.

The weather is cooling a little because of the rain; typically, it starts cooling around this time; it has been a sweltering summer in South Georgia. Green all around, shrubs and grass are growing faster. It looked unkempt, I had not put myself to work on it because of work, and the boy who comes to do the yard and clean up outside has been out of town on a job. I do work a little in my small flower garden. Some company would do me good.

"How do you feel? Come, sit, would you like something to drink, the weather, although raining, is cooling," I said, turning to the girl, Maryann.

Through the years, the porch became my favorite place where I never feel alone; this place has been good to me, the sounds, the scents from flowers and grass and trees, the birds chirping, the woodpeckers became my waking call, new friends, work is fun and magical. Although worn and washed out thru time, there is an old set of chairs and tables; one can still observe its original design and grandeur somewhat lost, looking more brownish than white. I had found them in the back closed-in porch, now my workshop. After dusting and cleaning, I moved them to the front porch making the house welcoming. I have a bottle of lime juice fresh from the lime trees by the side of the house. I've been trying to keep the house's character intact in case Mr. Darwin would show up.

As I served Maryann some lime juice, she started questioning,

"Do you live alone? What's your name? What are you

doing here? Where is this place? The girl asked. I could tell her emotional state. Her words and attitude were from the streets. I softly and slowly replied, "I'm Lindsay; I live here; it's been my home for over three years; it belongs to Mr. Edward Darwin. He generously allowed me to have it, but I'm taking care of it, feeling he might come back". - *At least it's what I want to believe; I dream of meeting him one day*, I thought- "Yes," I added, "I live here alone. Well, no, with my friend smarty here," directing my eyes to Smarty, who was already sniffing her and trying to get her attention. "I have a small store in town. It's about 40 minutes away".

"You have asked me who I am and more. I believe I can ask the same, who are you? How did you end up at my door?" I softly asked, trying not to scare her.

The girl burst into tears, crying in rage, desperation, devastated, uttering, "I had to, I had to, I couldn't stay, it was insane. I just left. I walked thru town and kept walking to the next city for hours, avoiding the roads. When I got to the next city I bought a bus ticket east, for 8 hours, I couldn't see who sat next to me or looked out the window, I was too tired, and I slept until the bus stop, it was dawn, I got off. I didn't care where I was; I just wanted to get further and further. I went into a breakfast café and ordered toast and coffee, Paid after finishing, and left. I walked for about 2 hours, got to the train station, and bought a ticket to Georgia. Money was tight, sobbing kept on, waited at the train station for over two more hours and finally got on with just my bag pack kind of heavy with essentials and some money I had been saving and kept it hidden from Milton, it was from my tips. After a while, I finally realized I had left".

Trying to calm her by telling her to breathe and letting her know she was safe with me, I asked, "Why don't you start telling me your name "? Who did you leave? What? And Who is Milton?"

I could sense the girl was wary. However, she said, "I'm Maryann; Milton is my uncle; he and Mama Jean raised me after my parents died. I was 6, I don't remember them, and I hate them for dying and leaving me with Mama Jean and Milton". Maryann was around her early twenties, a pretty girl, easy to see a rough life through her eyes.

Lindsay asked, "Did they send you to school? –

"Only Until I started High School because I wasn't doing too good, and Milton put me out to work on the street. He kept offering my services to men and taking the money. He slapped my face; you have no idea! Last month I missed my period, did a house pregnancy test, and came out positive. I knew Milton would kill me, so I got guts, and after getting off the train somewhere in Georgia, I started walking down south thru dusted roads until a dead end. I slept two nights under longleaf pines, run out of water, I did go across a creek, and kept on going, thru shrubs, bushes, bugs, heat, I was giving up, I don't know how I made it here, plus I've been having nausea, vomits and I'm not feeling well". Maryann looked scared, as I was when I made it here three years ago.

"No need to worry; you'll be safe here. You can stay with me," I said.

We live in a bizarre world; why is this girl here? Just like me over three years ago. I wasn't running away. I managed to get out of the situation, which almost ruined my mental health, my life, and moved on to a better life finding a good place, amicable people, hospitality, kindness, and most importantly, friends. Is it a coincidence that Maryann is here? Is it my turn now to give a helping hand just like I had?

Coincidence! A second chance! A save! Maryann and I are escaping violence in our life, in our inner self, unhappiness makes you fight to seek a better life, and it is our choice how to seek a second chance. We find in our path the opportunity to choose the right one. It makes sense; let's laugh or cry; only time heals. Everything happens for a reason. Maryann helped me with dinner, she was quietly watching me set the table and then sat at the table, and we both ate. I talked to her about Whispers, and she asked questions about my work. I offered to teach her; she immediately responded, "I won't be able to do it."

"Well, take your time, Slowly, a day at a time. I can tell you that no one will force you to do anything you don't want to do. What about the baby?" I asked.

Maryann responded defensively, -"what about the baby? I want this baby, I'll protect this baby, I won't leave it as my parents did, I will love this baby", and tears just poured out of Maryann's eyes. It felt like years and years of tears held; pain and sadness went thru her at this moment. We finished our meal, washed the dishes, turned off the light, and to bed we went.

Drummer! Every morning, the best sound, I jump and stare out the window to get a glimpse of "drummer" flying away to find his worm somewhere else. There is something good in my life every morning. It's Sunday; the store is closed.

Fall is starting to show in the colors of the trees, and the cold mist telling you hot coffee will be great!

Maryann woke up too. We were both zipping coffee when the sounds of our magical bell grabbed our attention.

"Oh silly me," I said; with Maryann's arrival, I forgot about my fishing day with Jeff. Thru the years, Jeff and I have become close friends, plus we work together. His beautiful wood pieces displayed at the store attract many customers, and like me, he never stops creating new pieces. I introduced Maryann to him and encouraged her to come with us on the fishing trip. She was wary and decided to stay with Smarty, who for some reason kept following Maryann all the time, even sleeping by her feet, as if he knew her.

Jeff and I went on our fishing adventure, which has been going on for three years. It was relaxing; we always had some conversation to enjoy our fishing. I have become quite good at it. Not only that, once back home, I have something to add to my diversity of artwork on silk, landscaping, rivers, fishing. We both have the best season coming and lots of work ahead, so these fishing days do the work for us.

Our everyday life goes by, smoothly active, uninterrupted. Dinner became regular with Agnes, Michael, Johan, Aisha, with more friends tagging along. Aisha and I worked together and shared many things; it was gratifying to have her as a friend. She never cease to tease me about Jeff, but honestly, nothing has crossed my mind, except the good friend he is to me., we work together, we have dinners with our friends, we laugh and enjoy our time when we are together, and most of all he is always helping me when I need help. No need to change things. I have to say, I've become attached to Jeff; I miss him when he's not around, but I never thought of romance. Sometimes I feel mindful; he has never invited me to his home but didn't make any fuzz about it. Thought of it as something natural, he wanted to keep his privacy and space. Maintaining boundaries is exceptionally smart.

Back at home, this time, we didn't cook the fish by the river; we brought it back to share with Maryann. Smarty kept her busy while we were fishing. To my surprise, she was holding a rag doll; she found it and reminded her of one when she was little and always kept but looked worn out. –"Where did you find it? I had never seen it!" –

"Under one of the accent tables in the reading room, there was a secret drawer, it opened up when I touched it, and the doll was there," Maryann answered. I was confused, but I let it slip.

The leaves started falling, the wind and the rain brought a nice cold mist as the leaves gracefully fell like ballerinas dancing with the wind. It's the in-between the heat of summer and the freezing winter, pleasant. Maryann and I could still sit out on the porch with tea or coffee and laugh at everything. Maryann seemed to be adapting to the new ambiance. She came with me to the store several times, but she always finds enjoyment back in the house in the old tool shack for some strange reason. Maryann was full of surprises. I came back from the store one day, and she was sitting by the work table in the shack with a box full of oil scents, along with small clear plastic, mini funnels for bottle filling, small empty glass bottles; test strips; a bottle of alcohol; to me, it seemed like a whole kit for perfume mixing. By her side, a basket full of wildflowers. She had asked me if I didn't mind her being in the shack and using all that. I didn't know that was there, nor how to use it, so I told her I didn't mind.

One evening, we were sitting at the porch enjoying some lemonade and cookies; I asked Maryann about the tools she found. She replied, "I don't know; I keep dreaming about a lady mixing scents sitting at the shack and a little girl next to her just watching and playing at doing the same thing. While you were at the store one morning, I went to the shack, knowing where everything was".

Maryann and I became close and enjoyed our time together. Her pregnancy was going well and showing more and more. We started buying things for the baby and decorations. Jeff built a beautiful crib; he had become very attached to Maryann, encouraged her to value life. She interacted more at the store, learning the business, ordering online, shipping, handling, and greeting customers as I kept entertained in my art. Maryann also contributed to the store; she developed the art of scent candles and spent time in the shack creating them. Her life was turning 180 degrees for good. She took walks and got to meet people her age, she was timid and suspicious of everyone, but she was getting more confident as days went by and began to smile more and more and even more when we talked about her baby.

This week, I went with her to her Doctor's appointment, and she was unexpectedly surprised by the ultrasound and Dr. Travis asked her, "would you like to know the gender?" she giggled and said timidly, "Yes, Dr. Travis, I want to see the baby, listen to the heart." We witnessed the heartbeats and then the words from Dr. Travis, "It's a boy." Maryann's eyes shined like stars; her happy excitement and tears of joy were inevitable. Like all this unexpected adventure, it was magical that brought me to Darwin's plantation. Thinking about Edward Darwin always gave me a strange feeling, as if he was part of my life, in between pleasure and fear. On the way back, all we talked about was the baby's room, the name, the color of the walls! Of course, blue became the color. I saw Maryann is laughing, happy, and contagiously happy. It was cold out, already February, and the baby's due date was May, only three months away.

And so, as the room waited for the baby to arrive, we started to welcome nice weather, birds chirping and flower blooming. I enjoyed fresh lemonade out on the porch when Maryann's water broke and a stabbing pain announced "Jasper" was on his way. We drove to the hospital and made it in time; Maryann went to labor, I was allowed to be in with her. For some reason, good or bad, I never got to experience motherhood. To me, this was some experience. Hours went by, her pain increased, the nurses kept coming in and out until the Doctor came in, reassuring us everything was coming as expected, and now it was Maryann's turn. I could only hear push, push and feel Maryann's pain as she held my hand tight, very tight until I listened to the baby cry and Maryann's hand loosen up. Jasper was now in her arms.

Life went on; visitors came in to meet Jasper. Cookies, pies, lemonade were in order all the time. Never missed a helping hand, a friendly neighbor, a good day. Oh! What a fairytale.

With the hunting season, business continued blooming every year, and life was good. Maryann spent her days between motherhood and her scent candle business and helping in the store with Jasper by her side. I continued my Sunday fishing day with Jeff, lovely days by the creek. Our friendship grew closer, as I did with Aisha, who kept insisting on something more than friendship between Jeff and me, and I always assured her it was not the case. My relationship with Robert and those terrible years I lived with him do not allow me to get emotional and think of anything more than a great friendship. I do admit I admire him; sometimes, I find myself, momentarily, staring at him with surprising enthusiasm.

Jasper was becoming a handsome, bright toddler, playing around all over the house. I found the reading room an excellent place for reading, especially on those rainy days or too hot, too cold to be out on the porch, and so it was on a pleasant day when Maryann was taking a nap, and I brought Little Jasper, now three into the reading room with me. He enjoyed riding on his toy car, around and around until the front wheels of his car got stuck on a loose floorboard, and Jasper started loudly crying, waking Maryann up and creating panic. What seemed to be a minor toddler incident turned out to be a little more than that—Maryann panicked when she saw blood in his arm. So we rushed to the hospital, which, as I suspected when we arrived, was a minor injury caused by a wood splinter that required a bandage and will heal on his own. We treated Jasper with ice cream on the ride back home, and he forgot everything.

It took a minor incident to work on the loosened wood

board that I had tripped over so many times. Not being my field of expertise, I called Jeff to the rescue. We were up for a surprise, like everything else since I arrived here! When Jeff lifted the floorboard, he noticed a box and pulled it out. We debated about opening the box, but in the end, we did. There were newspaper clips from a little girl's kidnapping in New Jersey back in 2001. According to the newspaper clips, when the family was back from vacation, Edward Darwin was holding the little girl's hand when his two sons, 14 and 16, got into a fight. He went to stop them and followed them inside the house; Mrs. Darwin was already in, and their daughter was left outside for a few minutes, not to see again. Sophie Marie, the little girl who had just turned six.

There was an investigation; the police searched for the girl and investigated delivery vans in service on the street that day, without luck. There was never a ransom request. No witnesses, no traces left behind. I could only imagine how devastating it should have been for them and why he chose to leave the house in Georgia. It probably brought memories of the last place they spent with the little girl. I wonder what became of the little girl. ? I asked Jeff to put the box back where we found it; maybe it was a way for Edward Darwin to try to heal, although, to me, it's an unbearable and unforgettable pain to endure. He put the box back where we found it, and the loose wooden board was no longer a danger for anyone.

These findings were the topic of conversation in our next dinner over at Agnes and Michael's. They were all surprised to hear that. They did notice Edward Darwin distanced his trips to the plantation. Once he came with the boys and stayed about a month; after that visit, he traveled alone and never brought Mrs. Darwin or Sophie Marie. He did continue going with the hunting team, but only to take pictures until he stopped coming. No one knew his whereabouts.

Nonetheless, I decided to research Edward Darwin, the mystery man, more to find out about the little girl than him. The mystery man stopped being one; when I read the news of the kidnapping, it left me with a sorrowful feeling for him. I wasn't intrigued by his character anymore.

This house is now my home, sheltering Maryann and little Jasper; I can't stop feeling the emptiness Edward Darwin felt in it. I valued every wall of this house, where I found peace, a new life with new friends, a family. It gave Maryann a sense of belonging; her dreams led her to find meaning in her life, creating scent candles and, most importantly, motherhood, a role she embraced so dearly, forgetting her past tormented life.

Maryann was very impressed when we mentioned the little girl's kidnapping eighteen years ago. She remembered she was six when her parents died, and she had to go with Mama Jean and Milton. "I can't remember their faces," Maryann said. "I'd make sure to stay safe and keep Jasper safe. He'll never be without a mother. And I will never let anyone hurt him". I guess we were all sad at the findings. That Friday night, Maryann had dreams. When she woke up and at breakfast before we all went to the store, Maryann told me she saw a lovely lady in her dreams, the lady would open the window in the reading room, and the wind would blow the curtains, she would run to let the soft curtains caress her face, enjoying the scent of the lime trees. The lady will hug her and say, what a delightful scent! She felt safe. There was something about the lime trees.

The day went on, we all went to the store. Maryann would sit in the back next to Jasper, who sat in his buster seat. It was a nice ride. We got to the store, as I was parking right in front of the store, Maryann became terrified by the sound made by a man who had parked his delivery van suddenly in front of us, slamming the back door, when he turned to look at us, Maryann started gasping for air, crying, scared. The man got on the van and drove away. It took a few minutes for Maryann to calm down.

"What happened, Maryann? I asked.

"I don't know, just got very scared," Maryann Replied.

Throughout the day, Maryann was quiet, greeting customers, and Jasper stayed in the classroom area, playing with colors. On the way back, Maryann mentioned that Milton always slammed the car door, and the sound of the man earlier when he banged the door brought terrible memories she had been trying to forget.

It was good that she was able to let it out, it helps in any healing process, and we have each other and good friends to keep our strength and the mystery of the quail plantation we both landed at, all in all, has led away to a new and better life.

Getting back to the house was always good; I always sat by the flower garden to contemplate its beauty and feel the ambiance invade me. It made me feel clean, fortunate, grateful, and appreciative of the good days. Sitting by the flower garden reaffirmed the garden in my soul, which exists inside and outside. Then thoughts of Edward Darwin's little girl came to mind, *how frightened she must have been, missing her mother and father at such a tender age. I wonder if she is still alive, what could have become of her and, What about Edward Darwin? Did he give up his search? or has he remained hopeful? His little girl disappeared in 2001 at age six; today, she would be 24, more or less Maryann's age, who also grew up without a mother and father in a much-tormented life.*

Life for Maryann has turned for the better; I care for her, trying to make her feel at home, feel that sense of belonging, and that Little Jasper has all the love and care to grow up healthy and loved. I suggested counseling to her many times; I told her how much counseling helped me at my worse moments until I finally decided to act. Maryann insisted she was okay; she also ran out, even if it was out of fear, feeling safe now, knowing there is a second chance in her life. Even if she doesn't know Jasper's father, she will always love him and care for him. Little Jasper made her leave the life she never chose to have. I didn't mention counseling again, so I focused on giving us a comfortable and healthy life.

That night, a noise woke me up in the middle of the night. I got up and went down; I noticed the door was open. I went back upstairs to check on Maryann and Little Jasper; Maryann wasn't in her room, so I turned the porch light on and went around the house calling Maryann out loud, and then by the tool shack, I heard a giggle, and smarty whining which led me to Maryann, she was hiding. I said, "Maryann! What are you doing?" she was acting like a little girl, in a little girl's voice, "shh shh, I'm hiding from Joy, we are playing hide and seek," Maryann replied. "Maryann!" I said in shock, what's going on? She then ran to the house. She had gone back to bed and back to sleep. I didn't know what to think. I couldn't get back to sleep, just thinking about the incident. *Whatever happened?*

The beautiful sky colors of pink, yellows mix with blue at dawn, what a lovely view, I went down to the kitchen very early to make coffee, sat at the porch, and that's how I came to admire the beautiful sunrise and listen to the chirping of the birds. This place never ceases to amaze me; it's an enchantment, it's magic; it just works wonders on me. Maryann interrupted my fairy dreams. "Good morning," she said; "you are up early for a Sunday. Are you and Jeff going fishing?" So after replying good morning, I asked her about the hide and seek game with Joy in the middle of the night. She had no idea of what I was talking about. I didn't insist.

Jeff arrived, and Jasper ran out to greet him. I greeted him too and asked Jasper to get his toy. Alone with Jeff, I mentioned what had occurred last night with Maryann. Like me, he didn't know what to think, we both knew she had a tormented life, she lost her parents at five or six but couldn't make anything out, and Maryann never agreed to therapy. Not only that, I don't remember ever mentioning joy's name. Ben, the mechanic, did say it to me on our ride to his shop in Thomasville.

Jeff thought it would be good to take them fishing with us. Jasper was delighted, and Maryann couldn't say no. Off we went; Maryann started singing a tune for Jasper and everyone followed. It was a fun ride to the park and then getting on the boat to the fishing area. Maryann felt she had been here before or a place like it. I love this place; it always has a relaxing effect, the stream flows, and it has a sweet sound when it touches the pebbles by the shore; the water is crystal clear, which made Jasper jump with excitement because he could see his feet in the water. Fishing by a creek requires silence; it lets you hear your surroundings, the sound of nature, and the flying fish making their splashback in the water. There's something so pure and peaceful about fly fishing on a small stream. The soft hum, the wind creaking through the trees, the bubbling ripples of the water, in other words, the sound of nature doesn't leave room for much noise.

The silence was interrupted by Jeff's catch and Jasper's excitement; what a happy little face, and Maryann's laugh was contagious. One after another thrown in the cooler until we started preparations for fish on the grill. It was a delightful day.

Chapter 5

THE SEARCH FOR THE FATHER

ACK HOME FROM A GREAT OUTING BY THE RIVER, AS JEFF predicted, the fishing day turned out to be fantastic for both Maryann and Little Jasper. We all took a shower, had a nice dinner, and Maryann put Little Jasper to sleep, who closed his eyes at the first line of the bedtime story. Both Maryann and I sat in the living room to watch TV shows. We came across a documentary on world-known photographers describing wildlife, nature scenes, and their lives traveling the world to capture the best they could, and it sure dragged our attention. It seemed very exciting to learn about men and women from different countries dedicating their lives to capture the world, the beauty of the earth, animals of all kinds, hunting, and more. It was then that images of hunting dogs came on. We were getting familiar with those beautiful dogs since living in quail land brought lots of hunters, and with the "hunting dogs." I made jokes on Smarty, who pulled his ears up as if he was understanding; he was a hunting breed but raised to be a friendly companion for kids as playmates. Maryann laughed loudly, and suddenly her laughter stopped as she stared at the image of the photographer. She then whispered "daddy" several times. I was startled when the presenter said his name, "Edward Darwin," from New Jersey.

All we have is Maryann's recollection of the image of her "daddy." *Was it real? Was it her imagination?* I think. Pieces were adding up one by one. There were things in the house which Maryann felt she had seen, but she didn't bother about it. The images in her dreams of a lady by the open window, finding the tools for scent making in the tool shack; the rag doll. I told Maryann we should see a professional for guidance.

Maryann always said she would never forgive her parents for leaving her, but the reality was, if what we both think about Mr. Darwin is true, her parents never left her behind. She did have a family who had looked for her; only she didn't know.

Our lives changed. Maryann was quiet and seemed worried, but we both sat and talked about what we should do. We decided, true or not, we should start looking for Maryann's father, becoming aware that I might get to meet Mr. Darwin. I did not know if that would make me happy or sad. It was time to start somewhere.

I couldn't sleep; I felt the need to start somewhere and didn't know-how. For the first time after taking the road all this adventure to Georgia, I think with no way out. *Is Maryann Edward Darwin's daughter? If so, what a coincidence we both find ourselves in this house, me not knowing who Edward is and*

Maryann, maybe, is finding who her father is. I am here now in a place that belongs to Edward Darwin, whom, I now know, is a well-known photographer; how hard could it be for me to find him and finally solve this mystery. Mr. Darwin might end up not only finding his lost daughter but also a grandchild.

My friend drummer, waking call, as soon as I opened my eyes, I repeatedly told myself, while brushing my teeth, showering, brewing coffee, in the car on the way to the store, "It's going to be a very, very productive day."

Maryann decided to stay, so I left; once again, I chose to drive thru the back road, where I can drive relaxed by the unspoiled landscape- Long Leaf pine forests and majestic live oaks draped with Spanish moss, which I can imagine by the sound of the river that runs close by the road. Sometimes the feeling and sound of nature make me set my projects and ideas in order. Today I need my mind clear and focus on locating Edward, listen to me, now "I'm referring to him as –Edward- as if he was a close friend, not even an acquaintance, nothing I don't know the man." Why do I get this shivering feeling whenever I think of him? Remembering the documentary, he does seem handsome. I wonder what year was the documentary filmed! Again, let's focus on finding "Edward."

My thoughts were interrupted by the entrance to town, now on my way closer to whispers. Aisha was at the store already, greeting me with her usual sweet and welcoming smile. She has been a great true friend, sharing all my ups and downs. Worked was, as usual, updating inventory, customers here and there, planning our participation in a new event, until at the end of the day; at that point, Aisha looked at me and said,

"Lindsay, something is bothering you, let's stop for a drink before going home." And, so we did. After telling her about my findings of Edward Darwin, I revealed the truth to her about my arrival at Darwin's plantation.

"I have to find him now" I must look for him. Where do I start?" I said.

Johan came to join us for a drink, and surprisingly Jeff too. After ordering a drink, both Johan and Jeff looked at Aisha and me, sensed something was going on, making Jeff ask, "What's going on, ladies?"

Aisha told them the whole line of events, from Lindsay's arrival at Edward's plantation to Maryann's whispering daddy, staring at the photographer Edward Darwin.

Unexpectedly, Jeff reacted upset; he said I had kept quiet to the fact that I had invaded someone else's property and went on saying it was a crime! I told him about the letter which gave me the right to stay there, to me it was a legal document. Johan and Aisha felt the same way. Jeff was left with resentment for my lack of trust towards him during all these years, seven to be exact, but he could change the subject to the issue at hand, to look for Edward.

Jeff's reaction and how he softly managed the situation without anger or violent attitude, nor blowing it out of proportion, made me feel safe and an emotional bliss invaded me, lowering the shield I had covered myself with for protection. Just a thrill which changed with the main topic looking for Edward. We all left the place. Jeff probably felt my anxiety at the findings and my disclosure of my secret because he gently put his arm over my shoulder as he walked me to the car, apologizing for his reaction and showing understanding of the situation. I couldn't but thank him for being there for me, which led me to open up about my long, disturbing relationship, which ended in divorce, and start a wonderful new life in Thomasville, where I feel good. He replied he always wondered what brought me here but didn't want to intrude, which he felt was mutual. By the car, we hugged and exchanged looks. Jeff said, let's think about everything tonight and try to make a plan to search and find Edward Darwin. Saying goodnight without wanting to, we went our separate ways for the night. I drove back home with a new feeling, a happy one. It made me remember a quote I read somewhere "And if I'm wrong, educate me but don't belittle me." Jeff's kindness of heart helped me realize warm-heartedness does exist; life it's not about violence and rage and rudeness when facing troublesome times. *Is this friendship moving on to a different road? What am I feeling?* I listened to music and sang along until I drove home. Smarty's barks and tail wiggling added to my emotions of the night.

Jasper was in bed already, and Maryann was waiting for me at the porch. She searched online for photographers under Edward Darwin's name and felt disappointed at the list. I told her Jeff, and I will be elaborating a plan for the search. At that point, I remembered the box with newspapers and clips of the kidnapping hidden in the reading room. So I ran to the room, followed by Maryann, asking, "What? What's on your mind? What did you remember?" I nervously told her Jeff, and I found a box the day Jasper felt in the reading room because he tripped with the loose wood on the floor.

"What does the box have to do with finding Edward?" Maryann asked.

"Edward's daughter, who we now think is you, was kidnapped 18 years ago. I never imagined it could very well be you. There are clips, notes, and newspaper clips from the date of the kidnapping and the investigation in the box, which led them nowhere," I anxiously replied.

"Wait," said Maryann, "are you telling me Milton Kidnapped me and my parents are not dead? And in tears, Mama Jean has no relation to me at all? I'm not Rita J".

"Rita J? Who is Rita J?" I asked.

"I grew up with the name Rita J; Maryann is the name which came to mind when I arrived here." She was in tears, devastated, resenting Milton, who did her work for his benefit, against her will. She had no other choice. I had to stay strong for her. I couldn't allow sadness and resentment to invade me. I embraced her as a daughter I never had. Maryann and Jasper are my families. I need to help them and be there for them. I made some tea and calmed her down. I convinced her there's something good in every day, and the day she arrived here was one of those days. She admitted her life changed for the good, and just as she said, she'll take care and love Jasper and will always hold his hand, and promised to be the best she could be to make it happen. It's a moment to be strong now. I'm taking the box from the floor and reading all the information. We need to be realistic; we are not sure you are the lost daughter, lots of coincidences, let's remain calm and hopeful. This time, as I started reading the notes and clips of the kidnapping, I shared them with Maryann. Pictures of the little girl just like one in the office room.

Photographs of Mr. and Mrs. Darwin brought tears to Maryann, remaining strong to read about the whole story and how it occurred.

She jumped up abruptly, saying, "No wonder I was in shock and frightened when I heard the delivery guy slamming the van's door that day in front of the store! I remember a man grabbed me and pulled me in the back of a van; it was dark, and I remember Milton; it was Milton who slammed the door; he kept screaming, asking me to shut up. I had dropped my rag doll daddy gave me, and I went to pick it up when Milton grabbed me. I hit my head hard and held my doll tight. It's me; it's me! I'm not Rita J nor Maryann; I'm Sophie, Sophie, Sophie Marie".

"I must have slept long; when I woke up, I was with Mamma Jane, and she told me mommy and daddy had an accident and died. I don't remember any brothers, just two boys bothering me and taking my doll. They never let me play with them. Never saw them again".

"Maryann, or maybe I should call you Sophie; let's go to bed; it's late, we need to rest." I went to bed after a nice shower, laid on bed with a smile on my face remembering Jeff's soft words and his deep sweet look. Every night, I fell asleep looking at the chandelier up in the ceiling, waking up by drummer and the birds chirping. Looking out the window at my small garden, it was in bloom, the sun was coming out, and I felt full of energy. I ran down to brew coffee, and once ready, I went to my garden. Watering the plants, taking a few weeds out here and there, and nice morning breeze, feeling grateful, I sat on the concrete bench nicely placed to observe the flowers, listen to the sound of nature and feed my soul with good thoughts. As I sipped my coffee, I felt a warm hand on my shoulder; I turned to see Jeff. He had gone in the house, served himself a cup of coffee, and came to join me in my morning ritual. We said good morning with a sweet smile.

He made some calls to friends in New Jersey and reporters he had met during his active life as an architect. Most importantly, the editor of a New Jersey newspaper, known for highlighting family tragedies and following their stories. Hopefully, someone would get back to him. I told him of my conversation and findings with Maryann or Sophie's memories of the event that day in 2001. I also mentioned I went thru the box we had found under the floor. We should look at the clips; maybe we could see the newspaper or date leading us to Darwin's whereabouts. We had a good breakfast; Maryann and Jasper decided to tag along to the store with me. I still have a store to run and work ahead. The art with silk work in my home workshop in the evenings has been on hold, and we have a festival coming soon! Those nights playing with my silk have always helped me regain my strength and stay focused and copping with all struggles I might have in my life. Jeff is also working on some orders and went back to his work not without asking me to join him for dinner at his house. With a wink and a smile and feeling blushed, I accepted. It was the first time in over five years.

We all went thru the day, working, busy and me, excited about dinner that evening. Back home, Maryann couldn't but notice my excitement getting ready. Kissing Jasper goodbye, I drove off to my date.

I walk into this quiet, neutral home. The palpable mood of tranquility extends to the interior. In addition to finely tailored seating in linen, the rooms are sparing with Scandinavian furnishings and other midcentury pieces. Surprised by a line of beautiful indoor plants, I walked to it only to find hidden open stairs behind them going down! Curious, I dared to ask, "where do these stairs lead?" Well, no other than Jeff's secret hideaway, his wooden workshop faces a carefully designed patio, incorporating it to the exterior.

"I'm a daydreamer," he said.

"I've spent countless moments staring out at the tree outside my window, thinking as its waxy green leaves blowing in the breeze, but above all else, it's a great place to daydream. The more time I spent in my backyard—reading, snacking, and just dreaming —the more I started to picture what it could be instead. So, I accommodated a dining table and a fountain that glitters in the sun. A tiny garden made everything more livable, essentially envisioning a room that felt calm, along with the smell of wood emanated from my process works." Jeff added.

The concrete patio had geometric pavers extending nearly the entire backyard length. A small dining set and the sitting area surrounding a fire pit, a vertical garden, matched the surrounding greenery and some grass in the side yard, leading and connecting to the natural open space of the land. I amazingly nestled in a quiet, peaceful place with lots of trees and breathing space. "It is my favorite place, right outside my workshop, where I spend hours, days, and nights."

We went back upstairs to the open space area of the kitchen and dining room where Jeff impressed me with his cooking skills with appetizers and wine in between his cooking which led to a delicious diner in a beautiful set table overlooking the outside thru a big glass window.

Thru diner, we talked, and Jeff let me into his architect life and experience in the past and how he decided to leave the life of a successful architect to come to the quail land in Georgia. He had a professional life and became famous thru his works which led him into an elite social life. He met his deceased wife, a glamourous socialite enchanted by money and a frivolous group of friends, who disgusted him, trying to avoid social events causing problems to their lives together as a married couple. His wife ended going to the social events by herself, excess drinking, and even drug addiction which led to a traffic accident driving under the influence.

His wife died in the accident, and sadly he learned she died of the injuries sustained and highly overdosed, and there was a man with her who he discovered had been her lover for some time. After that tragedy, Jeff decided to sell his business and retire. He ended up buying this land and took refuge in designing and building this beautiful cottage, slowly polishing his works as a wood artist and offering woodwork services. At that point, we had gone down to the seats by the fire pit with some wine and while he held my hands, thank me for coming into his life which helped him find peace through his art in wood; it has been so rewarding realizing life is good. I told him it was mutual for his support and friendship all these years. We embraced sweetly; it was very heartfelt.

It had been a great evening, it was getting late, and he said, "by the way, Lindsay, my friend, got back to me with some names and phone numbers that could help find Edward. Let's work on that tomorrow". We kissed good night, and since then, our lives have changed for the best, getting us closer and closer and sharing more time, along with Maryann and Jasper.

Six months later, the search led me to Edward Darwin. I found his phone number and address. It was March 2019. Maryann and I were together in the reading room, and I placed the call; I put it on speaker when he answered.

"Hello, is this Edward Darwin?" I said.

"Yes, who is this?" It was a strong voice.

"My name is Lindsay Reed; I'm calling from Thomasville, Georgia. I asked, do you own a small plantation near Thomasville, Darwin's plantation?" I asked.

After a brief silence, he replied, "yes, but I haven't been there in years. Why?"

"Well, sir, I have been living at your house since 2012. I found your letter in the drawer, on your desk," I said.

Another brief silence. "What made you call me now?. Are you taking care of the house? What do you want?" the voice, assumable Edward Darwin, replied.

"Sir, I also tripped into a loose wooden board on the reading room floor and came across a box you left." I nervously added,

His voice turned hard, saying, "And? What do you want?"

"I want to travel to meet you in person; your daughter may be alive with me," I said.

"What makes you think so? It's been 18 years!" He sounded upset.

"Well, sir, I'd like to travel there with Maryann, whom I believe could be your daughter, and give you details."

He replied, "Before you do that, tell me what makes you think so, and I'll get back to you. I will not cover any expenses".

I gave him details of Maryann's arrival, followed by the events. A doll she found in a secret place, the scent-making kit in the back shack, the reaction to the man slamming the van door, the Milton and mamma Jean story, and the documentary she recognized him as her daddy. More importantly, she remembered when she went to pick up the rag doll her daddy had given her, and Milton grabbed her and threw her into the van.

"I'll get back to you!" and he ended the call.

Maryann and I were anxious and uncertain, with some bitter feeling. We've taken the first step, "Maryann, let's stay positive. He'll call, you'll see". I said to her, hopeful.

He did call, indeed! The following day, it was a Thursday morning. He didn't sound like the voice I was expecting to hear. I was expecting a friendly, excited, happy one, but instead, it was harsh, skeptical very distrustful. He didn't ask to speak to Maryann. Before we attempted to make many trips, he had called law enforcement, who we should be waiting for, to investigate and take DNA testing. I was suddenly in a panic, frightened, asking myself, would I be in danger because I'm on his property? Would I be convicted for trespassing? This time it was Maryann comforting me, reassuring me. "I am Sophie Marie!"

I called Jeff and Aisha. Jeff came immediately, Aisha stayed tending the store. The day felt very long; Jeff, Maryann, and

I talked about many hypothetical scenarios of what we would face trying to stay positive and realizing we had done the right thing.

We were seated on the porch when we heard a car driving in. It was a government car, and a man and a woman, nicely dressed, got off. The man showed an FBI id and the woman a public health badge. It didn't surprise me. After my conversation with Mr. Darwin, we all knew there would be consequences, investigations, proof needed, not just my word, nor Maryann, who could or could not be the child kidnapped long ago.

Agent James McCoy from the FBI showed his badge and identified himself and the Social worker from Public health. Agent McCoy wore a dark suit and tie, extremely formal. He asked for me specifically, and Jeff came out first to introduce himself, me, and Maryann. Following the region's hospitality, I invited everyone inside, offered lime juice, and asked them to sit. Agent McCoy went on to say; I hope you all understand that we are here to investigate a kidnapping dated 2001. Mr. Edward Darwin informed us that you, Ms. Lindsay have information on the case. I interrupted by stating that I didn't have information on the subject but did have a good reason to believe Maryann was the kidnapped daughter of Mr. Edward.

And, that's why we are here. Agent McCoy introduced Rachel Girdharl, a social worker from Public Health; she is with me to take a DNA paternity testing to get to the truth. At this same time in New Jersey, Mr. Darwin is having the test taken. Agent McCoy explained the process; The DNA test will be by collecting buccal (cheek) cells found inside a person's cheek using a buccal or cheek swab. These swabs have wooden or plastic stick handles with cotton on the synthetic tip. In this case, Ms. Girdharl will rub the inside of Maryann's cheek to collect as many buccal cells as possible, which we will send to a laboratory for testing. The alleged father and daughter samples will determine the results.

Should the test results be positive, You, Ms. Lindsay, and Maryann will have to travel with me to New Jersey, where the kidnapping occurred and the investigation opened.

And so it was. Days later, the result came back. Edward called telling us Maryann's name is confirmed, Sophie Marie Darwin, the girl kidnapped 18 years ago in front of Darwin's house in New Jersey. Sophie asked to talk to him, so I gave her the phone.

"Daddy, I remember you when I saw you on TV; it's me, Daddy, Sophie."

"Edward replied, "I never gave up hope; you are coming home."

"Where is mommy? I want to talk to her". Sophie asked. There was a silence. "You have a grandson."

"I'll be sending tickets for you, your son, and Lindsay," Edward said.

We got ready to travel. I didn't think I should go, but Maryann insisted and understood I could help them. Jeff was concerned about me going and just said, come back as soon as you can. Aisha and I would tend "Whispers," I'll take Smarty with me. We said -"see you later"- with a very heartfelt hug and a sweet soft kiss.

It was a quiet flight; Jasper slept the 3 hours to Newark, NJ, where Edward waited for Agent McCoy and us. Once in the airport and exiting the security doors to the passenger exit, Maryann let go of Jasper's hand, holding me with his other hand, and walked towards a man standing by the exit rail, holding a rag doll. By the moment she stood right in front and close to the man, Maryann couldn't keep her tears; they both embraced for a long time without words. Agent McCoy walked towards Jasper and me. He had been standing next to the man, whom I then realized was Edward Darwin; after the greetings and introducing Jasper to his grandfather, we all left the airport. I sat in the front seat next to Agent McCoy while Maryann and Jasper sat in the rear with Edward. I was feeling slightly awkward, not finding words to break the ice. Edward gave me a cold greeting at the airport, not even a thank you, after all, I had to unravel this encounter, but it was Agent McCoy who broke the silence.

"Ms. Lindsay, Sophie Marie's brothers Richard and William have filed a claim against you. When we get to the house, you'll have to accompany me to the station for questioning".

I turned to look at him in shock – "For what? What reason could they have to accuse me of anything but bringing Maryann to her Dad?"

Maryann was upset, screaming, "That's not possible; Lindsay has nothing to do with what happened to me. She has not been anything but a mother to me," and at this point, she burst into tears, and looking straight at Edward, she asked, "Where is my mother?"

"Your mother died a few years after your disappearance; she couldn't bear losing you," Edward replied.

This car ride from the airport to Edward's home had

nothing but black clouds. The gentle rain down in the beautiful Quails land of Georgia now seems like a dream shattered. I never imagined something like this, an unexpected situation. Suddenly Edward Darwin became a disappointment to me. I couldn't understand how he could have allowed his sons, Sophie Marie's brothers, to signal me as a Suspect.

The news of Edward Darwin's daughter found was out, and the front of his house was full of reporters at our arrival. I tried to hide my face as I got out of the car, Jasper was scared, and Maryann couldn't stop crying and saying, "Lindsay, let's go back home!".

I tried to calm Maryann down, telling her things would be alright. They will not find anything to support this unfortunate situation. I embraced her, whispering, "Maryann, my young friend, you are like a daughter, and Jasper is my grandson. Rest assured, knowing I'll come back to see you before I go back home. You are now with your family". Both Maryann and Jasper clenched to me. I softly got loose and waved goodbye to them as I left with Agent McCoy.

I called Jeff when I arrived at the station. I realized how much I miss him and need him by my side. I was not afraid, there was no reason to be, but I was sad and disappointed. I built a fairy tale, and there is not such a thing.

Edward Darwin, who at one point was an illusion, shattered into tiny pieces and brought me back to real life, true friends, true feelings long wished for showing me, it is never too late to feel alive. Jeff had only words of encouragement and, most importantly, reassuring me He would be waiting for me.

I learned Maryann would have to testify too. Sadly, I also

learned that Richard and William Darwin accused me due to the reward money offered back when the kidnapping occurred.

My interrogatory was long and tiresome. The detective questioned me, trying to find some trace of evidence, but there was none. I was in another place, another life, and only met Maryann when she arrived scared and lost at the doorsteps of the house I encountered by accident. Coincidence brought us together.

Sophie Marie came to the station to give her testimony, and there was nothing to support the claim against me. The case will remain open until they find the kidnapper, already known as Milton.

Before heading back to Thomasville, Mr. Darwin apologized to me and invited me to his house for a few days. I intended to talk to him about the house in Georgia and come to some kind of arrangement for me to stay until I find another place.

Edward Darwin's house had a quiet ambiance. I was able to rest while Edward entertained Jasper and Maryann. I looked out the window towards the backyard; it looked well maintained, but it lacked a woman's touch. I could tell Edward doesn't use half of the house but knows where everything was. He never remarried, and at this point, I am not curious to find out about his life as I did back at Quail land. Noise and laughs brought me back, Edward's daughters-in-law were in the kitchen fixing diner, and the boys and the children were around Sophie and Jasper.

At one point, Sophie went to the kitchen, offering her help to Emily and Katie. They had already served themselves some wine, and Sophie and I joined in. I was dazed by Katie's sarcastic humor when she asked me, "So Lindsay, what do you think of Edward? He's an available bachelor and around your alley. I would say!" I savored enjoying my zip of wine and just ignored her, turning to Sophie, "excellent wine, right?" I said. Giggling, "sure is! Let's enjoy it," Sophie said.

The men had beer, and Edward served himself a scotch.

The girls set the table, and dinner is ready. We were sitting around the table, me, in the middle, Richard and William with their wives and children. Richard and Emily had their seven-year-old boy, Robert. William and Katie, a five-year-old boy, Steve, and a two-year-old girl, Nicole. Jasper was not alone. He now has cousins. There were some tense moments when one of the girls, in this case, Emily, with a glance of sarcasm, very common indeed, brought up the subject of the reward money.

"It is not my intention to collect any reward monies. I had no idea there was one," I told them; William interrupted, "but surely, you are interested in the house!" he said. I saw daggers coming from every angle; all I wanted was to go back to the peaceful life and the place where I found out that it's never too late to have a real life.

Edward raised his glass and toast "to Sophie Marie, who is back with us after 18 years. We have to make it up to her and Jasper and you Lindsay, thank you for all you have done for her. As for the house Lindsay, as I wrote in the letter I left to be found, where I clearly stated, *It is my wish that the house serves as shelter for someone who can tend to it and make it a home. I honestly wish that whoever you might be can be fortunate enough to value and care for it.* I am happy it was you who found it. Tomorrow will start the process to transfer the title to you".

"You are very generous Edward, I would prefer you transfer the title to Sophie Marie; it could be her vacation home. Don't you think so, Sophie?" I said, looking at Sophie. It was the first time I addressed her as Sophie.

"And you can certainly stay there in our home. You can still enjoy the breeze sitting by your garden with your glass of wine". "It will make me very happy, and I know Jasper and I will talk father into visiting," Sophie Marie replied, which brought a smile to Edward's face. More like the face I had expected.

Not everything that shines is gold! I thought, as the rest of the family, not including Edward and Sophie, disagreed with Edward's plans. As the boys starter their arguments, Edward said, "You have no saying in this matter. In 18 years, you never mentioned any interest in it. I have made my decision. The plantation will be in Sophie Marie's name. It's for her to decide if Lindsay stays. I am sure we all know the answer. Sophie didn't know anything about the owner of the house. She found refuge in her own home. Doesn't it mean anything to you?"

Chapter 6

MILTON

⁓

THINGS AT DARWIN'S HOUSE WERE BEGINNING TO SETTLE down; daughter and grandson brought smiles to Edward's face. It was time for me to plan my trip back to my own life.

Edward had been very amicable, somewhat sweet, and gentle at times, proudly showing me some of his photographs of the hunting dogs and the quail land. His cold welcoming and the silence to his boys' accusation shattered the expectations I had of him. I don't know what I was thinking! I had mixed feelings about him. I should know by now that expectations about someone you don't know can lead to disappointment. Sophie Marie distracted me from my thoughts, all nervous, anxious, in panic.

She had gone out for a walk while Jasper took a nap. There is an inviting park close by with tracks for joggers and people to walk, and Sophie took a liking to that. She came into the room telling me in despair and tears, whispering –"Milton is here, Milton found me!".

"What?" I'm terrified; "how's that? Are you sure?"

In tears, "Milton followed me to the park, cutting right in front of me as I walked by the tracks. Of course, he was very intimidating; he grabbed me by my arm very hard. I asked him to let go of my arm; he was hurting me".

Sophie went on, "I don't know what to do, Lindsay. I'm afraid. I don't think he knows about Jasper, but all I know is that he wants money. Milton said he was not going to let me go that easy. He said I owed him, supported me, spent a lot on me, and is payback time. I got myself a rich daddy and that Momma Jane needs me".

"How did he ever find you, Sophie?" I said in hesitation.

Sophie cried desperately; "he told me he saw me in the news when he was at a bar and immediately took off to come here."

"Sophie, try to calm down" as I continued saying, "I understand how frightened you might feel, but we need to be smart and leave it to the police. It would be wise to call agent McCoy", but we can't let Milton get away!".

At this point, I didn't know how Edward nor the family would react to this unexpected situation. Sophie Marie hasn't shared her darkest moments about Milton mistreating her; most importantly, how he forced her to work out in the streets and give him the money she received. She was afraid her father would now reject her because of the life Milton imposed on her.

"Maryann, don't be so hard on yourself; it was not your choice," I said.

I can't help calling her Sophie; she became Maryann, my

daughter. My heart aches to see her devastated, losing hope when everything is falling back in place to have an everyday life, a family, to forget the dark cloud over her 18 years with Milton and Mamma Jane.

I will not let this happen; I have not moved away from every obstacle in my road to a new life to allow myself to stand still and leave my Maryann to fall back to Milton's outrageous demands. After all, Milton committed a horrendous crime and must pay for it. I firmly believe I have to do something against people like Milton. People must know they cannot get away, unacceptable.

Sophie Marie fell to sleep after I gave her a cup of soothing tea. I first called agent McCoy asking him to come because Sophie had seen Milton, the Kidnapper.

After my conversation with Agent McCoy, I called Jeff, who has always been there for me. He immediately answered and asked, "are you ready to come back?" After seconds of silence and a deep sigh, I shared with him Maryann's encounter with Milton in detail.

–"That's no good," he replied and kept on; "you should not deal with this situation alone, call the police!" I reassured him of my intention to take matters into my hands.

"I called agent McCoy already; he said he is on his way."

It was comforting to hear Jeff's voice and have his support; *he gives me strength*! So now I had to deal with giving Edward this new development.

To my misfortune, Emily and Katie had dropped by to visit with the kids. I wanted to avoid letting them into the details, knowing how cruel and nasty both of them could be.

There is nothing I can do now, I thought. Agent McCoy will soon be here, and I'm sure it will bring about many questions about Milton. Not a doubt in my mind, they will conspire with Richard and William, not so much about Milton but Maryann. I was not going to bother myself with that; I needed to talk to Edward.

After the hellos and answering their unpleasant questioning about my plans to go back to Georgia and Maryann's whereabouts, I asked Edward if he could spare me a few minutes. Emily and Katie looked at each other with wicked eyes, as if I was after him or his money. I ignored them, and both Edward and I walked into his reading-office room.

I didn't know how to start, my words didn't seem to come out, and Edward was getting anxious. Finally, words came out, and I was blunt, telling him, "Milton, the Kidnapper harassed Sophie when she was walking by the park, threatening and demanding money, and because of that, I called agent McCoy who would be coming shortly."

As expected, Edward reacted in rage, accusing me I had no right to undermine his role as Sophie's father. Adding I should have talked to him before deciding to call McCoy. We got into a somewhat heated argument when I tried to explain there shouldn't be time to waste. "Milton is a criminal, a dangerous man, and must be stopped," I told Edward. It was tough to talk to Edward, but I felt he needed to know what Milton did to Sophie. I was about to say to him when Sophie came in. She embraced me and said – "Don't worry, Lindsay, I'll tell him everything." Sophie told Edward what Milton forced her to do, leaving Edward in unbelief disturbed, holding Sophie in a heartfelt hug saying – "my dear Sophie, please forgive me for leaving you outside by yourself, it's my fault you had such a horrible life."

Emily interrupted us, who came in to let us know McCoy was here.

I could hear the kids playing in the living room as Emily made herself to the reading room, followed by McCoy and Katie. Katie, just bluntly outspoken, "something terrible must be happening for McCoy to be here." I turned to Katie and said, "I asked him to come because the Kidnapper is around." To be expected, the girls turned to me in a suspicious look; "well, someone must have informed him Sophie is here," Katie said.

Agent McCoy then directed his questioning to Sophie, who was still in shock but cooperating with him. Milton had asked Sophie to get money out of Edward, and then they would run away. It was then when Sophie, in despair told him, she wouldn't do that, she would never go back to that life, and she would never allow her son to live the kind of life he made her live. Milton took advantage of the surprised news of Sophie's son to threaten her with kidnapping her son if she didn't get the money and come back with him. Otherwise, he will kidnap her son, ask for a ransom, or she will never see her son again.

"I have eyes on you, Rita J ... I know where you are." Those were Milton's words to Sophie. Those words are a good sign for McCoy, and, to him, the Kidnapper Milton was making a mistake in our favor. He was sure the FBI would soon have him.

They know he is in the area; he has contacted Sophie. The plan now was for Sophie not to go out, for everyone to act normal and go in their everyday routine. The Kidnapper would think Sophie has not alerted anyone of his presence, and she is probably scared and figuring out what to do. Milton would get impatient and would then make a move.

McCoy placed undercover agents at the park, on the street, landscapers working on the front and back yard, and a phone operator intercepting calls coming in, should the Kidnapper make phone contact.

"Dark clouds don't seem to leave," I whispered, both Sophie and me alone. We were naïve with too high expectations that it would be a happy occasion with a happily ever after and everyone to go in their paths. Oh, but what a disappointment; little did we know we would be facing so many turmoils since we found Edward Darwin. It is humiliating when they look at us as part of a conspiracy with the Kidnapper. Our lives were so different back at the plantation. I ended up using what if, what if, what if, something I'm against because it doesn't bring anything good or resolve anything. *What we are facing is real!* I kept thinking.

Emily and Katie decided to go home with their kids. I have to admit, it was a relief watching them go out thru the door. They only gossiped. I overheard Emily saying, "can you imagine! She doesn't even know who the father of Jasper is". Sophie couldn't seem to calm herself. She even suggested we should go back home. McCoy reassured her Milton had made a mistake to believe he still had powers over her, and his mistake would lead to his arrest.

Two days after initiating the operation, no calls have come in or signs of Milton, but the Kidnapper made a move as expected. An undercover agent, a jogger, noticed a man with Milton's description walking around the park and looking down the street leading to the house. The agent took a picture and sent it right away. Sophie Marie and I played with Jasper when agent McCoy brought the picture for Sophie to verify the identity. Sophie looked at the image, confirming it was Milton. McCoy gave the order, "suspect confirmed, and move in."

One of the agents walked towards Milton; he turned and noticed another agent saying in a loud voice and pointing a gun at him, "stop, FBI, walk slowly towards me with your hands in the air."

Milton started running, trying to get to his car; another agent called out, "stop!" But Milton kept running. At the house, we heard a shot and a voice in McCoy's radio, "suspect down, calling an ambulance, the suspect is still alive."

A few hours later, the agents left, the operation culminated. McCoy announced, "the suspect is on his way to the hospital alive"; Sophie Marie would have to go to the hospital to identify him, which, once confirmed, will lead to his arrest for the criminal charge of kidnapping.

I hugged Sophie when I heard McCoy saying Milton was alive on his way to the hospital. I felt she needed me. Sophie came into my life for a reason, I grew stronger for her, in a way, a daughter who lost her mother and a woman who never had a daughter, finding each other at one point in life, both running from an unwanted life to one with the hope of a better one.

Sophie cried on my shoulder, telling me, "I want to forget him; he had hurt and abused me, making me work out in the streets for men who mistreated me." I told her, "it's was time to heal, and to do that; it is essential to forgive to free yourself from bitterness. You don't need anger in your new life. Jasper needs you now".

"I know you are angry for everything Milton made you do, but it is time to let go of the life with Milton and Mamma Jane. To forgive them doesn't mean you are forgetting but growing stronger to a better life," I added.

Edward interrupted us, saying, "You and Jasper are safe with me. You both will have the life you deserve. I'll help you make up for all those years we lost".

The next day McCoy took Sophie to the hospital, Edward went with her. Once by Milton's bed, she looked at him; he could hardly open his eyes nor talk. Sophie said, "I forgive all the harm you caused, not only to me but to my father and my mother. My mother died because of what you did. No crime gets unpunished". Sophie looked at McCoy and said, "this man, Milton, kidnapped me when I was a little girl."

After over 18 years, the mystery surrounding Darwin's house's findings in quail land led Lindsay and Sophie to Edward. Edward then called the FBI and agent McCoy was re-assigned to the case; finally, The FBI reported the kidnapping of Sophie Marie solved. Milton went to prison in a wheelchair to pay for his crime. Father and daughter are together; it's time for them to move on with little Jasper.

I began to experience awkward moments when the family got together. I was out of place, and "home" was calling. I'm relying on Jeff and Aisha to look after my store; I know they do it from their heart, but I have to tend to it. The silk is waiting for me to grab the brushes, dyes, sponges and work on my creativity. Most importantly, friends are waiting; they are there on good and bad roads, supporting and sharing a pleasant and peaceful life.

As I started making my plans again to go back to my life down in quail land, I began to wonder; *I only see images of good things and friendly people amazingly in tone with my free spirit life. What a great choice I made years back when I decided on a new beginning; what I read here and there on social media and listen to talk shows on the radio is real: it's never too late! So it is, and so it goes! Never a dull moment,* and my wondering was interrupted by the loud talks from the kitchen. Emily and Katie were always hurting Sophie with their indiscreet comment about Sophie's life. How can people be so narrow-minded and hypocritical? I noticed when Edward is around, they address Sophie with certain courtesy, but when he is not present, they act rude, offensive, and disrespectful to her. Sophie tried to justify her life during the years she spent under Milton's abuse, and the more she explained to them the things he made her do, the more reason for them to be cruel in their comments.

I couldn't tolerate that kind of behavior. I spoke, "who are you to talk that way to Sophie? Do you have any idea what she had to face? Can you imagine a six-year-old girl finding herself in a dark place, without her mommy or daddy? She ended up in a strange place with a rude man and a nasty older woman saying her parents had an accident and died. Where is your sense of decency and compassion? You two have children; can you imagine one of your children in that situation? And, yes, she was forced to prostitute herself, not her choice; she didn't know any other way". I then realized, one cannot argue with empty-minded people, and there was no need to justify anything. Sophie is a better person who has learned the hard way, days may not be good, but there is always something that can help turn a life around to find the good thing every day.

I looked straight at Sophie and said, "you are you, a sweet girl, a mother who knows what it takes to be a good mother; your mother was not there, someone took the privilege of having her by your side as you grew up and she died because she couldn't bear not having you; you have a chance in life now. I want you to stand up for yourself to make this your home and be respected, or you can come back with me where you already have respect, love, and a future in a more friendly and peaceful environment".

Edward had been standing by the door and heard everything going on. He looked at Emily and Katie and said, "I think you better leave. This house is my house and Sophie's house, and you have to show some respect".

The girls left, grumbling on their way out. I apologized to Edward; after all, it wasn't my place, nor did I have any authority but the feeling I have for Sophie.

Edward replied, "no, Lindsay, I should be apologizing to you and my dear Sophie. I know very well how Emily and Katie can harm people with their comments. I will be here to protect Sophie and Jasper". I could understand Edward; he lost his little girl, missed 18 years of her life, lost his wife, overprotected the boys, who grew up to give more value to material things than feelings, and did not learn to be humble and kind. Sophie made some coffee and served some dessert, and we all went to the living room where Jasper had been playing with his mini cars. Jasper asked, "When are we going back to smarty? I miss him".

"We are staying here for a while," Sophie replied.

I flavored my slice of cheesecake, the thought of a key lime pie came to my mind; yum. I closed my eyes and pictured the lime trees by the porch. I don't think Edward had a feeling for the plantation the way I do; for him, it was a vacation spot; I value it as a home sweet home, where the heart is. The house in New Jersey doesn't feel warm, and I can see why; after his wife died, he kept the house with the two boys. He traveled around taking photographs leaving the boys to tend themselves who lacked the warmth of a mother. One by one, the boys got married; he was left alone with the house to himself after. I hope Sophie can bring the missing warmth back.

Edward looked at me, saying, "Lindsay, I often find you absent. Tell me, how did you end at the plantation?"

"I wouldn't know how to explain it; both Sophie and I arrived at the house the same way, stranded looking for a new beginning," I replied. After I said that, I briefly told him about my divorce, business, and moving to Georgia.

"In reality, it was the accident and me losing my memory temporarily that led me to your house, which saved my life. The place, the land, the people I met little by little captivated my free spirit. I fell in love with the character of Quail land, its people, the hospitality, and my business gives me a reason to keep moving forward".

Sophie got excited talking about the plantation and how she felt safe there. "I feel grateful," she said, "because I met Lindsay; not only that, I learned the art of creating scented candles in different forms and colors. Lindsay introduced me to a different world. I learned to appreciate life".

Edward changed slowly, from the moment we arrived, his attitude was cold and suspicious; *who could blame him!* I thought. He now seems gentle, grateful, and appreciative of recovering lost hope and having Sophie and Jasper with him, and as for me, meeting the man I envisioned in so many ways led me to a lonesome man whose suffering and the pain stopped him from moving on. I hope he finds in his heart to realize that it's never too late and he can always find meaning in life.

After a pleasant conversation and playing with Jasper, Sophie and I went to the kitchen, leaving grandpa getting closer to Jasper, a sweet, playful toddler.

I sat by the kitchen counter, allowing Sophie to take ownership of the stove, pots, and pans and surprise us with a delicious cousin learned by watching me cook back at the plantation. I served two glasses of wine, followed by chatting and giggling about good days. We also enjoyed face time with Jeff, who had smarty by him. He sounded happy to know we were having a pleasant time in the best place of any house, the kitchen.

"When are you coming back? Smarty is getting anxious!" Jeff asked. I lifted my glass and replied, "To smarty then! I'll be there soon. I think things are falling into place here; Sophie and Edward are bonding".

Dinner was ready; Sophie called Edward and Jasper to the table. At the same time, Edward got a call from William. I observed his reaction; it was an upsetting conversation.

Indeed Emily told him his father asked her to leave the house. It felt like a never-ending situation. Sophie's return did not seem a happy occasion for the boys. How can she ever heal? I suggested to both Edward and Sophie the importance of therapy to help Sophie adapt to her new life and heal Milton and Mamma Jane's scars. Emily and Katie were not helping, neither William nor Richard.

We tried to remain calm and enjoy diner. It was good. Edward held Sophie's hand and said, "your mother would have been proud of you."

She smiled and said, "once Jasper goes to childcare, you can teach me how to take good pictures."

"Good idea," he replied. "It's time for Jasper to have friends, and you can start meeting other moms and socializing."

I added, "don't forget your scented candle craftwork; you can keep at it and send them to me." Looking at Edward, I said, "how about you? I can display some of your photos at the store. I understand you have a hunting dog's collection. I'm sure all the lodges in the area would love to decorate the walls for guests to admire". Laughter followed.

"Lindsay, you are not only a talented artist but quite a sales lady; I would be honored if you stay longer, and I'm sure Sophie will agree," Edward said. "You can't leave, grandma!" it was Jasper. I couldn't help watery eyes. "I can't extend my visit aloud; I'm not planning on letting go of the scenery I found down south which has captivated me," I told Edward. This time Edward was holding my hand; Sophie contemplated with pleasure, as he said, "Lindsay, you have no idea how I feel, knowing it was you, who found the letter and decided to make the house your home. I'm deeply grateful you brought Sophie back to me; I wish you could stay and be part of us". I didn't know what to think and where this was heading, but I couldn't help to blush and say, "I must go back; it is your turn to look after them. You can visit me, and the beauty of the quail land, which I don't think has changed; I'm sure Sophie will tell you all about it".

Chapter 7

BACK "HOME"

THE CLOUDS WITH THE LIGHT OF THE SUN THRU THEM make a fantasy! Looking through the small window of the plane, I want to touch them. I breathe slowly, knowing my garden is waiting for me, and then Jeff will be there too. *Is it time for me to have someone by my side as I get older?* I'm thinking. Up to this moment, I didn't envision having someone by me to share dreams, waking up good friends. But, the days in Newark at Edward's house brought mixed feelings about getting old alone. I found in Edward a lonesome man, hidden in his work, traveling and slowly in the few days I was able to share with him at his house, I saw bliss of softness in his face, the joy brought by finding his lost daughter, and a grandson. I have learned to be independent, I feel happy with what I have, but I have not stopped to think about the years ahead. *Do I need to hold on to that last shred of hope and life and stop being afraid to have someone sharing my life and grow old together?*

Am I happy with what I have, or just content? What are my most joyful moments? Did I allow so many years in a tormented life to destroy the possibility to share a life? more thinking.

The blinking sound telling me to buckle my seat belt for landing brought me back to reality. A relieve feeling, my busy schedule, the messy workshop where I find everything quickly, and my time flies, but I get to see a finished project. I also emerged myself in updating my website, inventory. I am glad to have Aisha helping in the needy greedy of finances, invoicing, purchasing supplies, monthly expenses. Most importantly and highly needed, our happy hour's dinners, get together; with a smile, I got off the plane, picked up my luggage, and out the gate to meet Jeff, who was patiently waiting for me. I felt blushed, hiding my excitement for a 70ish-year-old as I hugged him, and he sweetly kissed my forehead, saying, "I missed you; great to have you back. I'll drive you home to unpack, rest, then try to catch up with emails and get ready; Agnes will be calling soon; for diner at their place. Everyone is anxious to hear your experience with the FBI and everything else; they won't let you leave anything out, so be prepared".

As we arrived at the entrance, Jeff said, "I drove by on my way to the airport to drop Smarty off, adding, by the way, how was your encounter with Edward?" In a sort of witty tone, "did he meet your expectations?"

I laughed; "please, Jeff! I was curious to meet the mystery man, not a "prince charming," but to answer your question, I found him cold and suspicious at my arrival. I guess his sons, guided by their respective wives, had poisoned him against me. After everything cleared me of any wrongdoing, he became more receptive, grateful he even asked me to stay"; it was my turn now to be witty; Jeff held my hand tight, and we just exchanged looks.

Smarty jumped and wiggled when I opened the door; I was so happy to see him. What a warm welcome; that's what I call a best friend. "I have no words to thank you, Jeff, Smarty, the house, the garden; I have to find a way to repay everything you do for me." Jeff replied, "You will; I know you will. Now, Lindsay, remember fall has started, we have art festivals on the way, and the quail hunting season will be open. It's our best time of the year. Dear Lindsay, your free spirit and creative energy have also enriched my spirit. I remember when you first hired me to do remodeling to what is now "whispers," you radiated enthusiasm, a great impetus to work, create, give life to everything you touch. Well, it has paid off; you brought life to me. In the past years, we lived autumn to its fullest. Autumn is here. We have to get ready to welcome the start of the Quail season, a favorite American pastime. Listen to me, as excited as you get when we get ready to make Whispers stand out. I include myself because I have to admit that my woodcraft has evolved through Whispers".

He is so right! It is our best time of the year. The weather is the best, and nature brings the best of colors, the beautiful foliage that attracts many people to the area. I'm sure the neighbors and friends share our excitement; hunting season brings more visitors to the site.

Dinner that night at Michael and Agnes' was very entertaining. Everyone made jokes about me being a suspect in the kidnapping of Edward's daughter and how it came out to be Maryann, the girl everyone adopted as a daughter. The subject took a significant part of the evening and then swift to quail hunting. Michael spoke very excitedly and invited me to a hunting day to understand the feeling and why so many visitors come during the hunting season. The invitation followed Michael's talkative lesson on hunting in this specific part of the region. The bobwhite quail, to be exact, a ground-dwelling bird; Michael went on saying how the sport is sacred in our history, "even you Lindsay, make beauty out of the sport, in your beautiful art, your silk throw pillows, screens, with quails, hunt dogs, the scenery. Look at our walls; most of the lodges in the area have art with quail hunting, dogs so highly praised; famous artists have painted the subject; there are books illustrated with quail hunting life. Many celebrities, dignitaries' even presidents have enjoyed peace and refuge in quail land, and not to say about writers finding delight in the sport, the dogs chasing after the prey".

Michael went on and on, everyone paying close attention. At the same time, I heard his voice fading as I imagined men connecting to nature, staying silent, feeling the scent of pine. Beautiful hunting dogs sniffing, and the men waiting for them to point to the prey with the tail straight, no barking for a moment, and suddenly something alerts the birds flying scare into the air. The men's adrenaline rush, getting ready for their hunt, and then the excitement while the dogs run to catch the prey and bring it back to his owner. It gave me, just like it did when I first met Michael, a bitter-sweet feeling. I thought of Edward, who only followed the hunting team to take photographs to display later in some magazine. A loud voice is saying —what a sport!

This time it was Agnes' turn; we all know how excited you get about quail hunting, more than a need like back in the days; it's a sport, a very entertaining one. You all go after a fast animal. Now, let's not forget about the best companion a hunter needs, the dog. When you talk about quail hunting, you have to talk about hunting dogs. Someone else added, and what about the gear? Laughter went on, and diner ended; it was another evening spent in good company with a lively group.

The lodgers in the area are getting ready for the hunting season, and Jeff suggested I should contact Edward; he might like the idea to come and take his camera equipment and go along with hunting parties. Sophie would probably like that too. It didn't seem a bad idea. It's been two years since Sophie reencounter her life with her father and siblings. Things with the boys in New Jersey and the wives reached an understanding and acceptance, which turned out for the best. The best part, Sophie was happy. As for me, it has been about eleven years since I ended up by the stairs of Edward's home, facing adversity of encounters and situations; I learned to go through all stepping stones with courage and determination. I have friends; I face the everyday ups and downs of running a business and hiring more people to help keep inventory in stock. With Jeff woodcraft and silk pieces, we expanded our line to major stores that added shipping and distribution employees. We also decided to cut down on festivals but did encourage our students to go at it. Life at the store was always fun. The house also took its toll, maintenance, repairs—my every day, along with spending days of leisure with Jeff. I kept wondering, have I reached the point in my life when there's nothing more to wish? I go to bed at night staring at the chandelier with no one by my side; some warmth might be a wish.

Back in NJ, Sophie never missed a day to chat with me, keeping me up to date with all of the new activities and Jasper's stories. She kept working on scented candles, getting better at them. The store always had her candles; She missed me and the life at "home"; Jasper was six now. I followed Jeff's advice and asked Sophie if they had any plans to come soon and mentioned the hunting season. Although happy having his daughter and grandson, Darwin had some freelance projects and travels, so they decided to wait for spring. That made their visit official!

Along with their visit, I had mixed feelings, the excitement of seeing them again, and then the "awkwardness" of being in their home, with rights or not, I invaded their property. How can I be a hostess? I started having anxiety issues, something telling me I should leave the house and look for my place. I felt everything moving fast around me; Smarty's bark was louder. I found myself making some hot soothing tea, trying to calm down, and went out to my garden where I always find refuge, recover the patience with myself, and learn to make good choices. I was absorbed in finding the calm within the chaos when Jeff sat by my side; he had gone in the house first, grabbed a cup of tea, sensing something was wrong, and said, "what is bothering you today, Lindsay?".

Jeff, dear Jeff, he is always next to me, reading through me. "Well, Jeff," I replied, "Sophie and Jasper are coming to visit. I should feel happy".

"Then, why aren't you happy?" Jeff asked.

I explained that I realized things were getting better for them as a family through Sophie's conversations. William and Richard have learned to appreciate Sophie during the past two years. She made her presence felt with kindness; they bonded, and the boys' wives have learned to understand the life Sophie endured and how she found courage and determination to become the woman she is.

"Now, the Darwin's, all of them, are planning to come down, as a family, to their home. I invaded their property. It's going to be awkward for me. I don't know what to think about this situation," I explain to Jeff.

"Lindsay," Jeff said, after listening quietly, "maybe this is your chance, your call. I think the moment has come, leave the house, let it be the vacation home they once had and take your belongings and move in with me, I'll build a workshop for you, and you'd get to grow your garden, you have the gift to give life to everything you touch. We can then plant some lime tress you like so much. We have walked together for some years now. I remember as if it was today how you hugged me with excitement the day you hired me to redesign your store furniture. We share friends, enjoy each other's company, so many things in common as well as respecting our lives and space. We are together most of the time; let's make it our home and enjoy the time we have left together. Think about it, Lindsay". *Am I afraid? What stops me?* I thought. Jeff got up; I have lots of work to do; we all do. We'll talk later.

Life went on in my daily activities, and so did Jeff, although he was quieter than usual, humming and whistling cheerfully.

We shared our diner's on Fridays at Agnes', Aisha's, the house's wherever it took us; never missing our Sundays' fishing and Jeff always asking, "Any news on Sophie's visit" and I replied, "she will let me know." Then Jeff asked, "Any plans? Have you thought about my proposal?" This time I said, "How could I say no to such a proposal? I need some more time".

"I'm not going anywhere," Jeff replied and added, "Neither is our house."

On a beautiful autumn Sunday, about one month after Sophie's call announcing their visit, Jeff and I went fishing; there was something about Jeff, happier than other Sunday, but we enjoyed our fishing as usual. The water was cold, but everything around us, the birds chirping, the foliage, the water hitting the rocks, the fling fish sound, gave a warm feeling. Nature as its best! Fishing was over, and we started packing. Jeff said he had a surprise for me, no cooking by the creek! As usual, excited by surprise, I went along.

The best part of my life and what has kept me thriving to achieve my goals is the lessons I get from nature. Watching the leaves falling, knowing the trees will lose all the leaves, the birds will start flying away because the snow will be fearful, but everything will come back when the spring hits, the branches of the trees will recover their leaves, the birds will fly around, build their nest, summer will be playful and green. I thrive on overcoming what comes to me; I take chances, letting opportunity and preparation meet, like nature. I broke my silence, "Jeff, this is a familiar road, is your surprise at your house?" Jeff smiled, saying, "-And, here we are, dear Lindsay!"

"We'll go straight to the back, where the fire pit is, and we'll clean and grill the fish as if we were by the creek," Jeff said excitedly. It sounded perfect!

We had a great time between laughing, eating, and enjoying the moment. Another lesson from life is learning from experience to become a better –self-, which Jeff and I did.

"It was indeed a great surprise!" I said, and Jeff replied, the surprise is yet to come. Follow me", and so I did.

We walked out of the backyard, following a small trail between longleaf pines and some space leading to a small cabin, *what looks like a cabin!* Two steps to a small porch and a sliding glass door. Jeff signaled for me to lead. I walked into an open room with shelves, a sink, big glass windows, one overlooking the longleaf pines and another to an open land space. "I'm surprised indeed; this looks perfect for a workshop!" I said, admiring it.

Jeff then said, "this door leads to another two short trails. The one to the right takes you to the open space. This open space, Lindsay, is waiting for you! It will be your garden, and I'll build a bench. The other trail, covered, goes to the house, knowing you wake up in the middle of the night to work".

Spring arrived, a hammering sound woke me up, I jumped out of bed, the drummer is here, what a great sound, my waking call is back, with it, the chirping, a wonderful breeze, spring is in the air. Perfect weather for the Darwin's; they will be here soon. It will be wonderful to see Jasper and Sophie again. Their vacation home awaits them. I made coffee, filled my mug, and went outside walking thru the covered trail Jeff built to sit on the bench by the flower garden; it's blooming. Jeff planted some lime trees giving

Printed in the United States
by Baker & Taylor Publisher Services

shade to the flower garden. Jeff came out; it started to rain, "April showers!" I said.

We are now sitting out on the porch outside my workshop, wrapped in a soft blanket, drinking warm coffee, looking at the rain; the animals are sheltered somewhere just like me. It feels good, as if everything stops, giving me time to watch the rain hitting the leaves, the rocks, creating puddles of water and thus the lovely sound which brings such a pleasant, restful air invading me. I whisper in Jeff's ear, "Life is good."

The End